Strange folk You'll Never Meet

A. A. Balaskovits

sfwp.com

Library of Congress Cataloging-in-Publication Data
Names: Balaskovits, A. A., author.
Title: Strange folk you'll never meet / A.A. Balaskovits.
Other titles: Strange folk you will never meet
Description: Santa Fe, NM : Santa Fe Writers Project, [2021] | Summary: "From A.A. Balaskovits, author of Magic for Unlucky Girls, this new collection of unusual, fabulist fiction leads you down strange paths for dark encounters with familiar fairy tales, odd people from history, and weirdos who may be living right next door. Among the characters in these bizarre stories, a starving beauty finds a beast who can save her village, a man eats everything in sight but is never full, a woman gives birth to bloody animal parts, and a daughter is forced to dance every night to the reenactment of her fathers' murder. These tales invite you to spend time with people who, in the maddest of circumstances, chew their way forward. With elements of psychological horror, sly humor, and the fantastic, these stories will burrow under your skin, haunt your dreams, and make you wonder what worlds lie just beyond that tiny hole in the wall"—Provided by publisher.
Identifiers: LCCN 2020049260 (print) | LCCN 2020049261 (ebook) | ISBN 9781951631130 (trade paperback) | ISBN 9781951631147 (ebook)
Subjects: GSAFD: Fantasy fiction. | Horror fiction. | LCGFT: Short stories.
Classification: LCC PS3602.A594 S77 2021 (print) | LCC PS3602.A594 (ebook) | DDC 813/.6—dc23
LC record available at https://lccn.loc.gov/2020049260
LC ebook record available at https://lccn.loc.gov/2020049261

Published by SFWP
369 Montezuma Ave. #350
Santa Fe, NM 87501
(505) 428-9045
www.sfwp.com

For Cassidy, Finnoula and Saoirse

All the weird and wonderful magic in the world comes in threes

Contents

The Tale of a Hungry Beauty

Some children are born believing that there are monsters under the bed, witching and wheedling their way from their dark confines towards the light of the sleeper's eyeballs. If they make it that far, past screams and parents armed with brooms, the monster will settle in the child's head and make a gallery of terror and wonder to keep them entertained for the rest of their lives. "It's only your imagination," parents tell their weeping children, frustrated at the bed wetting and screaming once the moon rises. But parents have forgotten that they have monsters living behind their eyes as well, and have long grown dull to the presence. For the children who grew up in the village surrounding the high tower on the top of the hill, they knew the monster did not wait under their beds or behind their eyes. It was biding its time.

Belle heard the stories of this monster from her father. Depending on the telling, the monster was as big as a house (which is why he needed to live in such a large place) or as thin as a piece of paper. It either had sharp teeth or a mouth full of bleeding gums, but regardless of what it looked like, all of the villagers were stuck with its looming presence, and occasionally it would creep out into the night and steal children from their beds to live in the castle with it.

"Is it lonely, then," Belle asked, "to steal such company?"

"Hungry, I imagine," her father said. He always made sure the windows were locked tight at night and placed sheets under the doorways, so if the monster made its journey down to their small home, it would not smell Belle's uneasy breath as she slept.

In the town there were rumblings from the residents that the bravest of the boys should go and kill the monster and share the spoils of the tower. The only thing that matched the intense discussion of what the monster must look like was what it kept locked away in its home: all manner of gold and silver and at least a handful of rubies, plus all the food and clear water in the world, which seemed even more valuable when the cold swept past their heads and the land refused to grow in winter. Each time the snow settled into its yearly fall, the people would grow hungry enough to arm themselves with pitchforks and hammers and gather at the local tavern to talk about raising the place and ending the monster once and for all, but they'd always had one drink for courage and another for secondary courage, and then one for young Peter's birthday which fell around the Holidays, and then another for old Tom who had died years ago, that good man with silver hair and a quick smile. Soon enough, it was morning and they were all head-sick, and so they went home to sleep it off and try again tomorrow, starting with one drink for courage.

Belle, her belly rumbling and her hands shaking, decided that since she didn't remember Tom that well and wasn't fond of drink anyway, she should be the one to make her way to the tower. Her father was withering and there was only so much she could sell of their meager possessions to have bread for the table. If she could not rely on the men to go and release the riches from the castle, then she was perfectly capable of it herself. When her father was in bed, tucked in with thin blankets and a cloth wrapped around his left hand where his thumb had rotted off last winter, she kissed his forehead and bade him pleasant dreams. She wore her heaviest coat and the shoes with only the beginnings of wear in the sole and went out into the night. She passed the tavern with the drunks and heard their war cries and, while they were not meant for her, she felt rallied by them all the same.

As she walked, she came across a huddle of old women who, curious to see someone walking towards the tower at such a time, or at all, asked her where she was going at this hour. When she told them, they crossed themselves and started to weep into their hands, which Belle thought was a bit much. They told her their own theories of the monster on the hill: it was not some demon or long-fanged beast (after all, no one had actually seen the thing) but could be a cursed royal who had done a bad thing, and the romantic loneliness of it all was his punishment.

"It's a shame," they told her, "to suffer for the mistakes of the past."

What else would we suffer for? she wondered, but all the same she said their words were true and bid them a good evening.

"Suffering is the great sin," they told her retreating body, but that only confused her more. What difference was suffering through a curse compared to suffering from hunger or a broken body? Her father had lost his favorite thumb to freezing last winter digging through the snow for a single root to boil and eat. He had not been able to find any roots, but Belle, clever as she was, used that thumb to make the stock for a thin soup that lasted them through the coldest days. After, over a drink and with a waggle of his remaining fingers, he told anyone who listened about how his hands staved off the starving. His hands and her practical mind.

Her own hands, she thought, were nothing special, but she looked down at the cracked skin and chewed nails and thought, well, at least they are clean. And attached.

When she made her way to the entrance to the tower, huffing with exertion, she collapsed at the doors. The sound of her body hitting the cold, old wood reverberated through. She only lay at the entrance for a few moments before the door creaked open a little, and two glowing, bleary eyes narrowed at her.

"What do you want?" a strangled voice asked her.

"Right now," Belle replied, "a fire to warm my toes. But I'll settle for a polite hello."

"Hello." The voice said gruffly. "Is that all you came for?"

Belle laughed at that. "I think I might freeze to death out here," she said, chattering her teeth.

The voice sighed, as if to really drive home the point that the girl was putting it out, and opened the door. If Belle had been warm, and her belly full of food, she may have had enough energy to express her horror at the monster before her, but as it was she was too cold and too hungry, and so could offer little more than a slight baring of her teeth at him. It was not the patched fur, like a dog with mange covering his whole body and face, or the thin, pointed horns jutting out of his head, or even his paunched belly sagging near the ground, his back hunched over by the weight, but his eyes were the color of gold and glinted so unnaturally, Belle felt revulsion on the back of her tongue.

He swept her up in his arms and carried her into the tower. Every room they passed, though it was sparsely decorated, had a fire roaring, and Belle felt more like herself the more the beast brought her deeper in. He deposited her, not entirely gently, on a bed so soft she thought she would fall into its middle and never make her way out.

"You're nothing more than skin and bones," the beast said to her. "You'll get one carrot and you will warm up and then you will leave."

"Is that all you can spare?" Belle asked. "A single carrot?"

"You didn't earn it," he told her, "so I am being more than generous." He left her, and Belle fell into a comfortable rest with nary a beast behind her eyelids. Later, when she awoke, there was a single carrot lying next to her on the bed, with the green stem and dirt still attached. She chomped on it spitefully.

She felt better with that little bit in her belly and decided this was all very much a lost and stupid cause. She decided to make her way into whatever corner he was stashing the food and stuff as much as she could in her dress pockets and bring it back to her father and the rest of the villagers to eat. It might not be much, for she had shallow pockets and thin arms, but it might, if they ration, be enough to make it through the winter.

Unfortunately, she did not know the direction of the kitchens or pantries and took to tiptoeing around so as not to run into him again. She found, instead of food, pictures depicting ancient battles and nude women so fat Belle could not believe they existed except in perverse imagination. She found creaking furniture covered in dust, and long tables with cobwebs. Whatever riches the townspeople imagined were here, well, they would have been disappointed if they ever managed to stay sober enough to make the climb.

She did, however, find a library, or a room that was supposed to be one, but now had more shelves than books. The ones that were left were very old, and when she attempted to lift up the cover of one particularly large text, it blew up enough dust to make her cough.

"You're still here," the monster said, grumbling and looming behind her.

"Yes," she said, because that was a true statement.

He seemed, for a moment, like he wanted to rip her head off and be done with the whole mess, but instead he looked over at the book she had tried to open, and narrowed his eyes. "You know how to read," he said.

"No," she said, because that was a false statement. "But my father knows how to, and he would read to me. I like the pictures. He had only one book, you see. I'm not sure where he got it. I suppose he bought it when I was younger and we had a little extra money, before the winters became so cold. It's a book about cakes, you see, all sorts of cakes. One of the pictures is of a cake so large it is bigger than the women who baked it!"

"You won't like my books," he said.

"No pictures?" she asked.

"There are pictures," he said slowly.

"Well," she said, feeling a challenge. "Show me."

She supposed she should be shocked at the depictions in the first book he showed her, but she had seen such things in person, and so this historical treatise about how to dispose of the dead did not shock her so much as make her think it was, perhaps, a little out of date, for no one oiled the body and set it on fire anymore. What a waste of grease.

"These don't bother you?" he said, and Belle could hear the awe in his voice.

Why would you want to live with what terrified you, she thought, instead of filling your home with what comforts you? Yet she stayed quiet as he told her how these books frightened him, how he used to lay awake and dream of death and starvation and all manner of horrors, and so he collected these books and forced himself to look at the pictures to numb himself to it, but it only made it worse, and so he stopped looking entirely, and they had gone to waste in this room.

"It's nothing I have not seen already with my own eyes," she said.

"Of course," he said, his gold eyes large and focused on her. "I suppose now you'll want more of my food."

Thinking this was his way of asking her to get out, she said she would be happy to leave, and thank you for the hospitality, such as it was, though the hunger aching in her belly indicated this was a lie.

"I suppose it's too cold for you to go out now. You'll only make it halfway and then you'll freeze to death," he took a long sniff at her head, so long Belle felt uncomfortable at his closeness. "You smell like you're about to croak as it is. And then I'm sure some rugged man is going to come here and blame me for it," he said. "Which is all very inconvenient."

Belle agreed it was, though having known all the rugged men in her town, also knew that they were too hungry to make the climb. That evening, he fed her an onion.

Their first days together went very much the same as their next. Belle would look for where he stashed the food and come up empty. The beast would grumble at her presence and give her a single vegetable, or an apple or a pear, but only one, at night, and then herded her to the room he had dropped her the first night. Sometimes, he would stand around her, making conversation about the pictures on his walls or the drawings in the books, and asking her what it was like to not be afraid of dead bodies. She didn't know how to respond, and said it was something you just get used to, she supposed. She started to tell him the story of her father's missing thumb, to return the favor of shared dead parts, but he only moaned and covered his furry ears.

Eventually, she knew she had to return home. Her father must be worried about her. Yet, when she went to the front doors and bid the monster a stiff farewell, the turnip he had given her secured away in a pocket, she was surprised to find that he did not want her to leave, even barricading himself against the door and waving a stalk of celery in her face if she agreed to stay with him.

She didn't really want to, but it had been ages since she tasted fresh celery.

He took to waiting outside of her door in the mornings, shadowing her steps even as she searched every room of his vast tower to figure out where he was squirreling away the food. He would read to her, like her father had done, and wait for her to react to every page, offering her a single green bean pod if she did. Since she was hungry, she reacted every time. He asked her what she wanted beyond food. Having always been a person who had needs, not wants, she was confused by the question. So, he asked her instead: what do you like to do when you have free time? What would you like to do if you had no worries in the world? Where would you go if you had nothing tying you down? What would you see if your eyes could behold anything in this world? She thought these questions ridiculous, and only laughed at him for thinking to ask.

One day, he presented her with a little chocolate cake, and when the sugar touched her lips she cried.

"I have something else for you," the beast told her, and she hoped that it was another sugary delight, but the way he was holding his hands behind himself indicated that, if he had a cake or any sort of baked good, it would have been crushed. Instead, it was a ruby on a gold chain, a fairly large ruby, and as beautiful as a little sparrow's heart.

"That's very nice," said Belle, taking it and admiring it against the light. "What do you think this is worth?"

The beast rumbled before her. "Worth? It is worth worlds. Kings of all nations would lay down their lives to gift this to their queens."

"Really," said Belle, distracted. "I think I can sell this at market. Not ours, mind, but two days walk from town there's a field where the merchants from all over exchange their wares. Think of all the flour I could buy with this. We could all make bread for years."

The beast snatched the ruby out of her hands and put it in his mouth. With an exaggerated performance, he held Belle's furious hands away from himself and ignored her shrieks of displeasure, then swallowed it with a gulp.

"What did you do that for!"

"If you are not going to appreciate a gift for what it is when it is offered, then you don't deserve it."

"But it could be so much more," she argued.

He would have none of her protests, and even though she tried every trick at her disposal, crying, begging, arguing with cold logic, he refused to be moved. She even tried reminding him about her father and his missing thumb, and how devastated she would be if he had to eat the rest of his fingers. The beast told her this did not matter to him, for he did not know the man, and why should he care if others did not have what he toiled to gain? Really, it was she who was being unfair, asking this of him.

That night, when it was especially cold, she shivered in the bed, though the blankets were heavy and warm. The beast was waiting in the shadowed corner of the room, and at the sound of her teeth chattering, he crawled into bed at her backside, the great big, furred lot of him, and wrapped himself around her.

"I don't want to," she started, but did not know how to finish.

He only rumbled beside her, appearing content that she was there, if nothing more.

She fell asleep then, warm in his embrace, but she dreamed of her father gnawing on his limbs, and when she awoke her eyes burned from the salt collected there. The beast was still wrapped around her, snoring into her neck. She placed her hands on either side of his face and smoothed the fur around the horns atop his head. His eyes, when he was sleeping, did not repulse her. She wondered what a monster thought about his own kind, and if he too looked under the bed before he slept to search out his cousins and friends.

No, she thought. A monster does not look for its own kind. The monster of a monster is already in its own head. They were born there, take root and grow like corn.

She remembered that she was the daughter of a man who could eat his own thumb to stay alive: what other lesson could she possibly need to know how to defeat monsters? You do strange things to survive.

She would find out what his monster looked like.

She curled her lean fingers into claws and licked the edges of her nails. They were dull, but stronger now that she'd eaten onions. Carefully, she pressed the pad of her thumbs on his eyelids and pressed down with all of her strength.

Oh, how he thrashed, how he wailed under her! But she held on, grateful that she had all ten of her fingers still, and that her thumbs were the strongest of them all.

When he was silent under her, and his chest no longer rose with breath, she removed her fingers from those sockets and dropped his eyes to the ground. Before they even bounced, gold flew out of the new holes on his face, piles of it, coins and statues and jewels on delicate chains, so much wealth, it was enough to trade for generations, and everyone in town could have enough. But she did not stop there. With her teeth she tore open his large belly, and out poured chicken stock and flour and onions and pomegranates and potatoes and carrots and celery and beef hearts: so much food, she knew she would fatten up everyone enough to last this winter, and each after that.

With a cry of joy, she ran, blood on her hands and mouth, to the front doors of the tower. She opened them wide and shouted out to the town below her: there is food here, there is gold here, there are enough bones to make stock for months.

Slow, but sure, the townspeople climbed the hill to meet her. When they saw the body of the beast, and so much food, and so many precious stones, they began to dance. Whirling and twirling one another, they danced until their feet were sore, and then they began to prepare the heart of the monster: the first meal they would all be able to eat together.

The Mother Left Behind

She did not know when the hole appeared in the eastern corner of her daughter's room. It started out small, and she thought they had mice. She told her husband to fix it, but when he did not and it grew larger, she assumed it was rats and called the exterminator. When they found nothing alive but filled it up with caulk to make her happy, she thought that was the end of it, but the hole was there the next morning, and bigger still. She tried to cover it with tape, then wood and nails, and finally stone, but it remained, almost the size of a dog. Once it was large enough, each night her daughter went inside and disappeared, only to arrive downstairs the next morning at the breakfast table, covering her smiling mouth as she yawned. Her mother told her not to go into strange holes and moved the bookshelf in front of it, thinking that was the end of the affair. Yet, three nights ago she went into her daughter's room and found the bookshelf moved, her daughter's small suitcase gone, and a note with lopsided hearts left on the bed. Her daughter was nowhere to be found.

A life left leaves objects in the days after it disappears. The mother packed up her daughter's things and placed them, none too gently, into the large box that once stored their refrigerator. She threw in the trombone she had bought the girl when her interest had been music, following that with books when she thought the girl had been into stories, the ballet slippers when it had been dance, video games half played, sketchbooks half drawn in, cookies half baked, and a stuffed elephant half grimy, half clean.

"She was never good at anything," the mother said aloud. "Not even simple things, like staying in place."

Her husband, leaning in the doorway, said, "Yes, dear."

"She gets this from your side of the family."

"No one I knew ever went in a hole," he said.

The mother ignored him and placed an armload of dresses into the box. The white ones on top of pink on top of the green and red Christmas dress that was worn for half a day and was still stained with punch.

The mother grumbled when she dropped the dollhouse and the little plastic people fell on her foot. "What's so special about a hole in the wall, anyway?"

She packed school supplies, half used, and assignments half completed, which explained the C report cards. Then she tossed in a cheap Venetian mask with a crack near the eye. She packed the tea set and the rabbit made with real fur, now matted, then the poster of some group of teenage boys.

"What could possibly be in there that we haven't given her?"

In went crayons and markers and molding clay. Then the compact mirror, nail polish and lip gloss, a scarf, mittens, and a handheld fan.

"Are you just going to stand there?" she asked her husband. He put his hands up and left.

She placed the porcelain doll, with the eyes that shut when it was horizontal, purchased for her daughter on a whim, into the box. She had been saving it up for a Christmas gift. Untouched, unsullied, unused. She pushed the doll down to the bottom and heard its face crack. She panted and struggled, but through sheer spite the mother pushed all the half-used things from her daughter's half-life to the hole in the wall. One by one she lifted each object, spit on it, and threw it in. Hours later, there was nothing left but the box. That, too, she shoved in, punctuated with a curse on her daughter's ungrateful little head.

There was nothing in the room now except wallpaper, the bookshelf, the bed, and the mother. She stared at the hole for a long while, tracing her hand on the perimeter. Looking behind to make sure her husband was not loitering at the door, she took a deep breath and squeezed her upper body in. Her head, neck, arms and stomach fit in easily enough. Her hips and behind, large, obtuse, padded with teacakes and other sticky-sweet things, caught on the plaster. She took a deep breath and flexed her muscles, attempting to make herself smaller, and wedged her thighs closer into the outline. Panicked, she attempted to crawl out backwards, but her body would not budge, and she wailed and yelled for her husband, though if he was home he was making a point of ignoring her.

Somewhere in the darkness ahead of her, she heard her daughter's laughter, like a bright, ringing bell.

In the Belly
of the Bear

She was indigestible—this, a gift from her godmother, the one with bright eyes and brighter lips dancing around wine cups who blurted out her offering to the babe as she had no tangible offering in hand—this girl may be consumed but she will never pass.

It seemed like no true gift at all, until when she was older, past her bleeding, a bear all scruff and brown came upon her sleeping under an oak tree and gulped her whole. The swallowing was a quiet thing, and she did not awake until she was fully in its belly, tickled by the acids and disgusted by the stench. This is the end of me, she thought, and waited for her body to disintegrate in the juice. Yet, as time passed and the juices bubbled up against her skin, no part of her passed away. She remained snug and she remained warm and she remained.

Others came through: one, a grandmother whose hair fell out in clumps, gasping that she didn't want to die like this, a whole life dissolved away; another, a young boy who cried for his mommy and whom she could not shush nor comfort, though she laid her hand on his cheek and whispered all kindness before his skin bled to his bone. Then, another girl, like her, who peered at her with dark eyes and smiled, who grasped her hand and said she was happy that she would not be alone at the end of all things she knew. They brought their lips together and kept them pressed tight until there was nothing left of the other girl but those two strips of flesh. She balled her hands and beat at the belly after the girl had passed, but all she heard was a muffled roar.

Eventually the body of the bear stopped moving, and she continued to beat her fists against its belly, but though he grumbled and though he roared he would not give her a short-lived companion. Time was loneliness in the dark.

It was not until she heard voices, muffled and masculine and coming closer, that she was renewed with her desire for a friend, and she punched the belly again to wake the bear so it would eat. When he did not move, she brought her teeth to the slippery lining of the stomach and bit down.

How the bear moved then! Yet no matter how much it jumped and scratched at its own stomach, the girl continued to rip through the blubbery wall, spilling the acidic juice over his organs, and then she took to his grease-fat and his skin, tearing it open from the inside.

She emerged, covered in blood and yellow bile and slime. It was cold outside, and colder still were the expressions of two hunters, staring at her wetness like they were seeing a creature they could barely comprehend. She moved towards them with her hand outstretched, but they shied from her and crossed themselves. When she opened her mouth to speak, she dribbled acid onto the ground, and it smoked up around her. The men howled and clutched their axes and hunting knives to their chests and ran from her, screaming, "Hail Mary!" the whole way.

Only for a moment did she consider running after them, but it was so cold and she had no shoes, and so she returned to her bear, and clamored back into his belly to wait out the winter. Then, she decided, she would find those men who ran from her, and she would bite them, too.

The Mad Monk's Weeping Daughter

"When I signed my contract to dance," Mme Maria Rasputin said to me in fluent French, "I had no idea that I should have to dance to the tragedy of my father's life and death, and be brought face to face on the stage with actors who were impersonating him and his murderers. Every time I have to confront my father on stage a pang of poignant memory shoots through my heart, and I could break down and weep."

—'Mme Rasputin's Circus Ordeal', The Advertiser, Adelaide, Tuesday, February 19, 1929.

Six nights a week, Maria watched her father die under the hot, bright lights of the circus tent.

She knew of men who had seen too much bloodshed—those who investigated the murders of wives, the brothers who shot their cousins over nation states, and the kings who were beaten off their thrones and eaten by a starving populace—those men did not even blink at the bloody scenes, after a time. Yet, she always cried. Every night, except Sunday, which was a day for sleeping and drinking more than her regular allotment of water, she danced on her long legs in time with the thump of a small blade entering her father's stomach, and then twirled around him as he ate and drank poison on small tea plates, and rose and fell to the ground in a heap of tulle and lace with each gunshot—one red burst in the front, one in the back, and one square in his forehead. The man who played her father, Wilhelm, chosen for his ability to grow a long, scraggly beard and his particular cleverness in holding raspberry jam in his mouth until the final blast, where he then let it spill out between his lips in a curdled cry, did not quite look like her father. His eyes were too dull, liked faded coins, and he was not nearly as tall. But memory is memory, and a false one was as painful as the real. As they dropped a tied-up Wilhelm into the 'river', which due to the limitations of the Busch Circus' infrastructure, was only a small tub filled to the brim, Maria turned to face the audience so they could fully appreciate the salt running from her eyes.

This moment was what the managers called the show-stealer, and the only reason they kept her around long after the thrill of putting The Mad Monk Rasputin's Dancing Daughter! on posters lost its initial surge of curiosity and cash. The musicians swelled their sounds to a high pitched climax and a spotlight centered on her face as Maria stood still as stone, the only movement was the water on her cheeks, and the splash of Wilhelm surreptitiously being pulled out of the tub and a fake body being lowered in, face down. Wilhelm was, much to the managers dismay, not quite as clever at holding his breath, or climbing out of the tub with his hands tied to his body.

People did not flock to circuses to cry—no, they came for the laughter of clowns and the thrill of small, lithe bodies flipping in the air without a net to catch them—but all around Germany, men, women and their hiccuping children came primarily to see a daughter weep night after night for her lost father. They too, invariably, would tear up. Some audience members were quite proud and only wept a little at the corners of their eyes and dabbed away the water with handkerchiefs or sleeves. Others fully wept into their hands as if they could not bear to look at her for one more moment. Some never looked away from her, and growled with sorrow like a bear with its paw caught in a trap.

All of them, when asked on the way out if they enjoyed the show, breathed a little easier, a little more clearly, as if their sympathetic sorrow was what they had been yearning for, even if they did not know they yearned at all.

"You never fake it?" Wilhelm once asked her after a show as he gingerly wrung the bathwater out of his hair. He passed her a small towel for her face; her makeup always ran. "Not even once?"

"I am a dancer," she told him. "Not an actress."

He smiled at her in a way that showed all of his teeth, even the black, rotting one in the back of his mouth, and she did not know if she had given him the answer he was looking for, or even if it was the truth.

* * *

Maria was not the greatest dancer in the company; that title was held by Gerda, a small woman with blond hair and pointed toes who made the mistake of aging out of a rather reputable ballet company. Gerda never quite made principal, though she did understudy for the lead once or twice. But the circus was a place of exaggeration, and on her placard she was toasted as the finest little ballerina across the Atlantic, even though she had never traveled overseas. Even so, Gerda's ability to stretch her legs into a perfect line in the air was no match for the power of Maria's tears to move a crowd.

"Who you are is what brings them into the seats," the tall manager with a mustache told her. "It is because you cry that they stay for the show."

"Have you considered being his widow?" the short, stocky, bare-faced manager asked her with the same casualness one uses to ask a stranger if they are waiting in a queue at a bakery. "The mad monk's weeping widow. Now that's a hot ticket."

She refused them, much to their obvious dismay, but as she was the star there was little they could do to change her mind. Instead they asked Gerda, who was three years younger than her, to play the role of Rasputin's wife. Their logic was, if one woman could bring a tent that sat two hundred to tears with her face alone, what could the power of two women do?

They sold out the show before noon the next day.

* * *

That first night, Maria almost refused to dance, but the managers waved the contract she'd signed in front of her like it had power over each pointed step she took, and it did.

"It's harder than I imagined," she begged them. "I thought I could do this."

"Fraulein," they told her, "even those who do not believe in themselves need to eat."

It helped to see Wilhelm up close, because no one with two eyes could mistake him for her real father. The way his eyes did not crease when he smiled, his blue eyes, the way his nose was far too small, even with the help of the costume department, who tried to fill it out with clay; this was not the man who would take her outside to look at the bright lights above them on cool nights. Surely, a paying audience would see through the ruse and leave disgusted.

But that audience, and subsequent ones, did not leave. The first few laughed at Wilhelm's poor acting; his mimicking being poisoned left much to be desired. It was as if he thought poisoning was akin to eating bad fish, the way he hunched over and tried to gag. The audience watched Maria dancing with the politeness of men held at gunpoint. When she faced them after Wilhelm was submerged, she felt how hot her face was and the wet slime of snot running from her nose. As she reached up to wipe it away—completely outside the choreography—she heard the first sniffle. Then another. Someone yelled, "My God!" and started to wail, and then they were all wailing.

It was enough to almost make her stop crying, though not quite. It felt good, that first show. They were crying with her. They were feeling the loss of her father for who he was, not what the papers and the politicians had made him out to be. They saw, through her, a man who was not some magician, but a common man in strange times. A man who loved her, and whose loss she would always feel.

She was content to walk out of the ring that night feeling, for the first time since she could remember, how wonderful it was to be among people.

Wilhelm visited her that night to congratulate her. The edges of his nose were an angry red where the clay hardened. "Were they crying for you?" he asked her. "Or were they crying for themselves?"

"I made them cry," she told him, grasping that sentence to her heart like a ruby. Yet, the next night, as she heard and saw the audience cry, she wondered who their tears were for.

* * *

Gerda and Wilhelm were the only ones with dry eyes during the performances, though Wilhelm could be forgiven as he ended up wet at the end of it, regardless. Gerda refused to look at her, much like she refused to don a dark wig to play a mother or any makeup to make her look older than she was. She said it would get in the way of her dancing.

"I should dance in front of you," Gerda said to Maria, though she was addressing the two managers who were shifting behind her. "Your grand jeté is too low."

Maria acquiesced to the demand easily; she didn't want to dance at all anymore and would not if her traitorous body did not require bread, meat and cheese. The managers were less than thrilled with the suggestion, but Maria left the three of them to argue alone, confident that they would let her know if the choreography changed.

She found Wilhelm outside the tent smoking a thin cigarette, wearing his costume. He offered her one but she refused. She'd never seen her father smoke.

"Gerda wants to dance in front of me," she told him, not because she liked talking to him, necessarily, but every time she heard his voice she was reminded that he is not my father.

"That's all wrong," he said. "She's beautiful, but people don't come to this place to see beautiful things. Here, look." He opened the tent flap a little, showing her the mismatched chairs of varying degrees of rotten wood littering the ground, and Gerda whipping her hands up into the air while the two managers attempted to placate. One of them was on his knees. "See the ground? It's dirt. That should tell you everything."

She told him it didn't tell her anything at all.

He let the flap fall and adjusted his clay nose. "Everything beautiful worth seeing is kept in beautiful places. Jewels? A velvet lined box. An opera singer with a voice as clear as glass? You'd sit on a fur lined chair on a marble floor for the pleasure."

"They come here to see…trash?" she asked.

Wilhelm shrugged. "An affordable joy. What they think their happiness is worth. But you give them something else." He said this with a sort of curiosity a cat would have for a sparrow fluttering before it. "What do you think that is?"

The managers came fumbling out of the tent flap, followed by a red-faced Gerda, who took one look at Maria and stomped off.

"Well," said the thin manager. "I would say that went well. Fraulein, we have reached a compromise."

"What do you think of polar bears?" the fat one asked.

* * *

In the end, Gerda danced behind her and, as a result, barely anyone looked at the girl in the back. Not when she was jumping in the air or twirling on one pointed toe. It was just as well. She danced like a doll that was thrown into the air by a cruel child. But Gerda was not the only performer off their game that evening. Wilhelm flubbed several of his lines, perhaps distracted by Gerda's laconic performance. Or maybe he stumbled because behind the audience in thirty rusted cages were great white bears in all manner of size. They humphed and moaned through the performance, sometimes so loudly that the men playing the executioners had to yell their parts.

"Why bears?" Maria asked Wilhelm.

"It's a circus," he said, as if that explained everything.

She understood why the managers had brought in the bears when she stepped into the circle for her first series of twirls. It was the symbol of her homeland, though those bears were brown (it's a circus, of course it is a little over the top, a little wrong around the edges). More than that, the audience was forced to weave between the cages to get to their seats, and those in the back row had the unfortunate effect of the smell and breath of the animal right next to their faces. It made them jumpy. It gave them pause. They came in feeling afraid.

"Marvelous, isn't it?" the short manager asked her after the performance, when the crowd was teetering into a frenzy. At least two of the audience members fainted—no matter, it was to be added to the advertisement—and one unfortunate mustached fellow released his bladder, which caused the bears to growl louder and slam their bodies at the cages. "Why come for just tears when you can have the whole range of emotion in one quick go?"

Maria, who had not stopped crying, only nodded.

* * *

One afternoon, Wilhelm asked Maria to join him for lunch, which she declined. It was not as fancy as when a man asks a woman outside the tent to spend an evening together. The circus ate together out of the same pot of perpetual stew, added to and regulated by a crass hunk of a woman who must have never tried her own dish with the amount of cigarette ash she'd let fall from the stick in her mouth. Maria never ate with them if she could help it. She would grab her bowl and walk to a secluded corner where she could eat and wipe her eyes away from her father. She walked to her corner only to find Wilhelm there, placing a half-clean towel on the dirt and uncorking a bottle of wine with his teeth. Wearing his costume.

"Sit," he said, indicating the half of the towel he was not taking up. Out of a desire not to eat with the others, and also not to give up her spot, she did.

He poured them each a bit of red wine in wooden cups and toasted her, even though she held the wine limply in her hand and then put it down once he was finished thanking mother Germany for her bounty.

"You were very good today," Wilhelm said to her. "I didn't know if you would reach everyone over the bears."

She carefully removed a suspicious black chunk from her bowl and put it on the ground for the ants. He looked like he wanted to say more, but discouraged by her silence, he started in on his own bowl, pouring himself another cup of wine.

She watched him while he ate out of the corner of her eye. Her father did not drink. Not in front of her.

As a child, she was not trained to be a dancer, but she danced as all little children do on any clean surface they can find. She did not jump into the graceful lines of the ballerina, nor did she tuck her body in half and stretch out of her legs like the Barynya dancers who entertained the Tsarina and her children. Instead, she moved as her body allowed her to, this way and that, arms stretched and then tucked and then stretched again, fingers waving at her father, who always laughed in his kind way when he told her that her movement was beautiful, no matter the tempo.

Her father did not drink. She did.

"Why do you never change?" she asked him. "Your costume," she clarified to his bemused hum.

"Do you not like it?" He asked her, winking as if he was sharing a private joke between the two of them.

She made quick work of her wine, gulping it down in one long swig and stood up. Wilhelm reached for her hand, but she was stopped by the strongman, a muscular beast of a person, chasing a huffing baby white bear across the field in front of them. The strongman shouted in several languages for it to stop, as though he believed if he tapped into the bear's vernacular, it would sit and wait.

"The cages are too rusty," Wilhelm said. "That's the second one that's gotten out."

"The second?" Maria asked, shocked enough to sit back down.

"Cheap metal and cheap seats," he said.

The strongman yelled in a language Maria did not recognize and, in a great exertion, flung himself on the bear. He wrestled with it, pinning its front paws to the ground and sitting his weight on the furry back. He grabbed it by the skin of its neck, as one might with a hissing cat, and walked with the struggling animal far in front of his body.

"He should be careful," Maria muttered. "If the managers see him, they will have him wrestling the adults."

* * *

That evening the tent was packed. The sweat of the men, women and children in the audience made the bears especially rowdy. Perhaps it was the wine, which Maria still felt swirling in her veins like a hot snake, but she started crying earlier than her cue. Wilhelm gagged over the poisoned tea cakes. He always bent down to do so, his hair falling in front of his face, and for a brief, terrible moment, Maria remembered her own mother tearing the newspaper out of her hands, the one that described, with an aching amount of titillated exclamation points, how the mad monk survived a poison that would have taken down at least twenty fully grown bears. Why, he must have had a stomach made entirely of gold and evil. How the newspaper delighted in the tale, almost jokingly saying it was a shame his forehead was not made of the same stuff to deflect bullets, for then he might not have been brought so low as to bloat in a river.

She fell to her knees and held her head in her hands, trying not to make a noise, trying to contain her grief so that it was hers, hers, hers alone, but she shook so hard her hands could not cover her, and she wept a high falsetto. Gerda, an artist, decided this was her moment, and danced so beautifully in front of Maria it would have warmed the skin of a man encased in ice, but the audience had no eyes for her. They yelled for her to move. One man was so distraught by not being able to see the crying woman he yanked the lit cigar from his mouth and threw it at Gerda, striking her arm. She yelped and backed away so the audience could see Maria on her knees.

"Show us your face!" they yelled to Maria. She shook her head back and forth, pressing the palms of her hands into her eyes. The audience rose to its feet, yelling at her to let them see, show them all of those tears and her dark brown eyes, the same eyes her father had. The bears threw themselves against the bars of their cages, a cacophony of men and metal.

It was Wilhelm who, gently, pried Maria's hands from her eyes. "You must look at them," he said. "They've come to see you."

There was a story her father once told her on a cool summer night about a young, beautiful boy who had been born into silk and bad blood. His veins were rotting from the inside out, and no matter how many doctors bled him, no matter how many mystics threw bones onto the floor and made the boy drink tinctures of lye and salt, his blood remained sick. Because of course it did; sometimes, the only way to heal someone is to leave them alone. She asked her father what eventually cured the little prince, and he said it was the boy's mother, who quietly wept at the foot of his bed, and made sure that no one else came into the room to disturb him.

Some grief must be left alone.

Yet she was not so lucky to be born into silk. She looked at the crowd who had come to disturb her. The crowd, even the bears, quieted themselves for a long moment; the time it takes for blood to move from brain to toe, and then she saw Wilhelm with a crease near his eyes, such a familiar crease, and his executioners raised their pistols to those eyes.

She screamed.

Screaming through the tears? Of course. A daughter can scream with water in her eyes, it is their great ability. She screamed for all those faded memories she knew no pantomime could ever accurately portray and no man in a wig could replace. The audience danced its own role alongside her, like a starving snake aching for its tail, and as she wailed they did too, and even the bears moaned. Did they hear her in Berlin? In Saint Petersburg? How far does the sound of loss travel?

The weeping went on for a very long time, that night. Even Gerda wailed.

Before he went into the bathwater, Wilhelm gave her a curious look, but his eyes were very dry.

* * *

It was Gerda who came to her after the managers left her that evening. The two men were both displeased and overjoyed by her performance, and the warring emotions did nothing attractive to their faces. She'd cried too soon, the screaming had not been approved, but really, who could argue with the results? Why, some people bought their tickets for tomorrow on their way out.

Gerda brought her a small cup of water and told her to drink it.

"Why are you being nice to me?" Maria asked, suspicious and worn out. Her own eyes stung from all the salt that leaked from them.

Gerda shrugged and rubbed her arm where the cigar left an ugly, red mark. "I had a sister," she said. She looked at Maria, as if this sentence explained everything, as though the past tense mattered the most, even more than the word sister. "I've never looked at you before, when you were up there. Well. I looked at your feet. Now I wish I had never looked up. If only I had stuffed my ears with cotton." She wiped at her eyes. "My throat hurts."

They drank water together, like any family would.

"Wilhelm asked after you," Gerda said.

* * *

Wilhelm's tent was smaller than hers, but that was no surprise. The only one larger than her own was the managers' and the strongman, and the latter's was only larger because he could hardly be expected to be contained in small spaces, unlike the polar bears. The inside was sparse, little more than a bed barely long enough for his frame, and a bit of extra room for a small dresser and folding chair, presumably for guests or for reading the slim volumes of poetry he kept piled on the floor. The only decoration was a small statue of the Pieta, except in this one, the artist crafted the Mother's face to look up towards the skies, her blank eyes wide and her lips parted in a dull, horrified wail. The statue was gray, except for the cheeks of the mother, which shined as though fingers had rubbed across the smooth stone there again and again.

She should not have been shocked to see him still in costume, and yet, like a windchime, it panged silver and raw.

"Why?" she asked, pointing at the robes and his hair. There was no energy in her for any additional words. Even the water Gerda had given her felt like it was drying up in her veins.

"Why not?" he returned, grinning too wide.

He asked her to have a seat, but she refused, edging towards the front of his tent, prepared to run back to her own and cultivate her pain like a private garden. He sat on his thin, narrow bed and pointed to the small folding chair. Like an obedient daughter, she sat on the edge.

"Why?" she asked him again.

What could he have said to shock a woman who was shocked every night of the week, save Sundays? He could have said he had no other clothing and she would have believed him. He could have said he was ordered to never change by the managers, to keep her in a constant state of turmoil to guarantee a good show. He could have articulated a fantasy of incest and even that would not have come as a surprise, not really.

Instead, he told her how he wanted to unlock her magic. That's what he called it.

"The sway you have over them," he said in a way that was both shy and breathless. "It is as if you don't even know what a circus is supposed to be." He chuckled, a dry noise. "When they come here and sit in those seats…they come to forget. To laugh a little. To be amazed at the strangeness of our bodies. But you? When they look at you, they look inside themselves. And they weep."

Maria shook her head. "No," she whispered. "No."

"I have to say my lines," he continued, as though she said nothing. "I never get a good look at you. I wonder what I would feel if I saw you with those tears on your face?"

He tilted his head to the side, and in the dim light of the tent he looked unlike himself. His blue eyes were not so bright. If she narrowed her eyes, then he could be her father. If she willed herself to pretend.

And why shouldn't she? For one evening, would it not be worthwhile to willingly pretend? For each night she was caught off guard by her father's brutal murder, even though she expected it, would it be so terrible to, just once, pretend the man she saw with red jam in his mouth was, in a private moment, her father, alive and well?

It was what her father always told her; be kind to all, even if they do not deserve it.

She did not know if she was being kind to herself or to him.

"My father called me Matryona," she said.

He said her name in a whisper, again and again. He placed the palm of his hand on her cheek when the first of her tears fell as if to cup them.

"He would tell me stories before I fell asleep," she said. "He liked to laugh."

"As any man does," Wilhelm said, looking at the wetness on his hand as if it was an odd substance.

She told him stories, through her tears, that she had never told another soul, not even her own mother. Those private moments between a father and child when he teaches her how the plants rest under the snow until it melts, and then burst through the ground towards the sun until they flower. How he taught her that suffering is temporary and must be endured.

Each word she uttered did little to move the lines on Wilhelm's face, and when the light reflected on the clay, she gulped down the last of her tears. His eyes were white and blue, not a touch of red.

Wilhelm hummed and touched his own dry cheeks. "Not even a sniffle," he said. "Perhaps you do not have any magic at all."

* * *

Gerda came to her before the next performance and offered Maria her powder. "It is nicer than what you use," she said. "I don't need it anymore."

"Anymore?" Maria asked.

Gerda nodded and bent down to adjust her slipper. "I have not seen my mother in many years. I will go to her. Before there is nothing to go to."

The managers came to Maria with a new poster: on it, an artist had painted her on the top of a polar bear, her arms spread wide, her hair draped across her breasts. All she wore on her body were the painted tears on her cheeks. Above her, and taking up most of the room, was Wilhelm's face, his blue eyes, looking down on her with a wild look, like a demon from a child's story.

"My father had brown eyes," she told them, because there were no words good enough to tell them how deeply she hated it.

"Oh," the thin one said. "Be that as it may, when they see Wilhelm they'll see his eyes are blue."

"It would ruin the realism," the fat one added.

They left her with the poster and a cup of water to make sure she would have enough liquid in her eyes for leaking.

The tent filled up that evening. With the word of a new show spreading—why, you'll cry, you'll scream, you'll feel—even those who swore they could only witness her weeping once came back to see what the fuss was all about. Many people had to clamor in the aisles. The bears swiped and growled at those unlucky enough to stand with their backs pressed to the cages.

Gerda and Maria took their spots on opposite ends of the dirt stage, bowed, and then twirled towards the center where Wilhelm rose his arms and cackled through the jam in his mouth. His executioners, in their faded princely garb, which should have been beautiful as all royalty, even pretenders, should be, stabbed a fake little knife into his belly.

The two women twirled towards the center of the room.

When Wilhelm opened his mouth to bite those poisoned sweets, Maria's vision blurred, but no matter how she spun and no matter what arrangement her feet made upon the ground, the water stayed in her eyes as if it were ice. The executioners lifted their guns to his stomach—BAM—and then to his forehead—BAM—but even then, not a single tear escaped. She could see the mismatched bodies of the managers squirm in their seats, but even furious blinking did little to move the water. The jam in Wilhelm's mouth splattered to the ground, but even as the executioners bound his body with rope she did not cry.

She heard the splash and faced the audience.

Dry, dried up Maria. No magic left.

A young voice, perhaps a child, cried out in the back of the crowd. Strange—it was usually the front of the audience that cried first. Maria felt her cheeks to see if the liquid was leaking and she did not feel it, but no, it was not a cry of sorrow that erupted from the back of the audience and spread to the front. A polar bear, a small one, had escaped from its rusted cage. Theirs was a cry of alarm.

Women gathered their children into their arms and men flew up onto their chairs, as if being slightly above the bear would protect their meaty bodies. The executioners ran into the back of the tent, pulling Gerda with them, even as the audience screamed at them to use their guns on the beast. Fools, the guns were not real, and they would be as useful at stopping a bear as a song. Maria sat still and watched its claws and teeth come dangerously close to her face—it was running straight at her—but the strongman jumped on the bear before it reached her. He put his beefy arm around its white neck and flexed until the beast whined and huffed. Its head fell to the ground, tongue waggling out. Maria was grateful the poor thing couldn't taste the dirt it was licking with all the times she and Gerda had stepped on it.

The only noise from the audience was the sigh of the managers in the back.

Once the bear was conspicuously dragged off the stage, the managers waved their hands at the executioners to come back and resume their roles. They snapped their fingers at Maria and motioned towards their faces, puckering their eyes and making exaggerated frowns.

She turned around to look at the false body of her father just as the executioners dragged in a breath of air as rough as stone. The three men dragged the body out of the water. Wilhelm never was any good at holding his breath, and the executioners were exceptionally good at tying knots.

When they lowered him to the ground, the soaking caused the clay on his nose to fall off, revealing a slightly bent nose, but thin. The true nose under all that falseness.

"Is this part of the show?" a woman in the audience asked in such a loud whisper it could be heard throughout.

She never looked at the photos of her father's body in the papers. First, her mother wouldn't let her, and then as she grew older Maria had no desire to have her memory tainted with how others saw him. When she looked at Wilhelm, she suspected her father must have looked a little bit like that; soaked, with red near his mouth.

The tent was silent. His executioners, suddenly thrust into the realization that they had lived up to their roles, however accidentally, looked at Maria with the pitiful longing of children who need their parents to tell them how to react. She turned from them and faced the audience and they, too, were holding their breath, staring at her, waiting for her tears, perhaps, or her screams. Waiting for the release from the indecision of response.

There was a feeling curled in her breast. Rather, she called it a feeling, but only because it pushed against her lungs the way sorrow did, but unlike sorrow it was light, like Gerda's pointed toes on the ground. This feeling was unfamiliar, like a childhood friend, the sort you remembered was a part of your life long ago but disappeared once the hair on your legs began to sprout. It curdled behind her eyes and in her throat, and she found that she had no desire to keep it inside.

She opened her mouth and giggled.

She turned to see the jam burbling around his lips and wondered how anyone could believe it was blood in his mouth. You could see the seeds.

Maria opened her mouth even wider and laughed. And laughed. And laughed.

Not a single voice in the crowd rose up to meet hers.

The Candy Children's Mother

I had to send them away. They were not children born of my belly. They came rushing out between some other woman's thighs, one right after the other. I was told she lost so much of her liquid that, as soon as they emerged, squalling in the air, she dried up, all broken apart, and pieces of her blew away with the gust of their father's grief. I had not known her, being so young myself when she died, barely out of my first bleeding, that when I was invited to her funeral, as we all were, such a tiny village we come from, I looked at the remains of her bones with the pity one has for any dead animal. I expressed the appropriate grief to the father, my eyes down and my lips trembling, but he must have seen something genuine in me, where there was none at all, that he asked my father if I would be a suitable replacement, and then put a bag of coins in my father's hand when he hesitated.

It was not so bad, at first. The children would not suckle from my breasts, but I warmed milk from the goat and dripped it into their mouths. They grew: the boy, Hansel, with his greedy appetite, and the girl, Gretel, long and thin like a branch, but with arms that knocked the china from the table if she did not get her way. They loved me, I suppose, as much as their father did, though when they saw my belly begin to expand, the rain forget to fall on our small garden of vegetables, and the goat dry up, the four of us knew what would happen: a fifth would devastate us, and two would have to go. We would all starve if we remained together. I have not been taught numbers as the men are, but even I know that three is less than five.

I have heard that once you go into the forest, you come back a changeling. Or you don't come back at all.

Gretel was awake that night. Our small house had only one room for sleeping, and so all of us dreamed together. Yet, with my belly protruding too noticeably to be mistaken for anything else, I climbed above their father and massaged his neck and behind his ear, as he likes. I pressed his hands to my belly and rejoiced at what we had created. I whispered that I would not die with its birth, for I was made of stronger things than dust.

It was difficult, after we finished, to fall asleep, for that daughter who was mine but not mine stared at me all night, the moon reflecting off her dark eyes.

They cried, of course, the boy more than the girl, for his emotions reflected his appetite, and he was capable of keeping neither in check. Their father cried as well when he held the door open, but I held my hand on my belly—my only bargaining chip—and he gave them a little bread and told them they were old enough to make their own way, though they were young, too young.

At night, I asked them to forgive me, though they were already gone.

I bore him my daughter and I did not die.

* * *

She suckles from my breast and squirms and laughs with all the happiness of a small thing. I see myself in her, that bit of myself that did not have to choose. With so few mouths to beg, the goat returns to its milk. We are saved.

Their father weeps for them, though quietly, as he knows it upsets me and my daughter. I don't voice what flows in my veins: I do not want them to come back, not my strong-armed daughter nor my voracious son. If they come back, it is I who will pay the price for saving us, I who will pay the price for desiring my own daughter over them, I who will pay the price for making the difficult decision, though it was his hand on the door. After a few months, I suspect they have died out there, and while I feel the ache of loss, I am also relieved that I will not suffer their retribution, even though they would be within their right.

Tonight, a little before the birth of the new year, I sit on the little landing with my daughter wrapped up against my breast, showing her snow for the first time. Two figures make their way towards the house. Rather, I smell them first, the sickly stench of rotten sugar clings to them like a death. The boy is so big he makes the earth shake with each step, and the girl, tall and thin as she always was, has a red glint in her eye, and her teeth, when they are near enough to see, are filed to uneven spikes.

They are almost upon me, and I hold my sweet baby daughter to my breast as I stand tall to receive them, these children that I have sacrificed to save my own, these children who are mine and not mine, these children who now sniff at my arms and neck, looking for the place to bite.

Match Girl

Her mother said, "Darling pie, your lips are made of sawdust." And on her tenth birthday her mother bought her matches to scrape across that skin, to keep her warm when a mother's love is buried in the earth. The girl's cheeks were made of wood. "A flawed design", Mommy said, "but you make do with what you are given." In the matchbox there were only five sticks. Five matches for five lives, and as each one burned, the girl was to remember what she saw. Remember what she'd want to keep. If she chose right, maybe she will learn something. Maybe she will stay warm forever. Her mother, perhaps knowing she was a woman who had given birth in a fairy tale, had done her duty to the narrative and died, so sad, and took all the wisdom and snide humor in her veins with her.

* * *

Strike one—a scene of a little bird. Common. A sparrow? No, too big. One of those starlings who carry the night sky on their backs. His feet were tied with fishing wire to a tree branch, beating his little wings as fast as the tap-tap-tap of his heart. Someone put him there, some creature with nimble fingers and a thumb. The bird was not alone, no, his little partner twitted from one branch to another, unwilling to leave her lover. Perhaps the bird thought if she shook the branch hard enough with her body she would shake him down, and he would be with her in their nest again. Little bird brain. She didn't know his legs were broken.

* * *

Sawdust-lips kicked the snow at her feet.

* * *

Strike two—a man stepped on an ant, and then he wept. He built a little mound to remember the ant, or perhaps to memorialize his carelessness, but it withered away with rain because he had built it out of sand. So he built a larger memorial, using fallen branches, but a large wind swept it away to sea one evening. When his friends asked him why he was weeping so often they, too, felt the loss of the little ant, and the guilt that they loved someone who had done something so thoughtlessly cruel. They petitioned the city to build a stone monument in the square, sculpted into legs and a long abdomen, and it was beautiful, for a time, but an earthquake ripped the ground in two, and the sculpture cracked. On and on, the whole town built more memories, and on and on they fell apart, until one day they constructed a steam tower to float over their heads with banners floating behind it, circling their homes and the courthouse. But they forgot to put enough grease in the engine and it collapsed in the middle of the city. It crashed on the heads of eight children playing red rover, red rover, won't you come over?

* * *

Wooden-cheeks curled her toes as they became numb.

* * *

Strike three—there was a girl who had just been ripped out of the belly of a wolf by a man with an oversize ax, but he'd nicked her face on one side, and on the other the acid in the belly marked her as half-digested. She ended up better than her grandmother, though, who came out without eyes, her jaw hinged off, and very, very dead. The woodsman brought home the bloody ax and the bloody girl, and because he once read that if you rescue a girl, she's yours to keep, he placed her in his basement, which is like a belly in a way, but much colder, much drier, and so very dark.

* * *

Darling-pie shivered.

* * *

Strike four—there was no image with this one, only a feeling that curdled in her belly like sour sausage, the sort of nausea one experiences when they have had nothing to eat for days, but they forget that a starving stomach must have only bland food to start, and they imagine lavish feasts of pudding and toffee and syrup dripping over the edge of stacked pancakes, the kind of food that settles like a stone in your gut, but there is no stone, there is only a hole, and no table exists for you to sit at, no fork for you to grasp. Your teeth have nothing to chew.

* * *

Ten-year-old growled. She, too, had not eaten in some time, and that was the sound her stomach made. None of these stories made her feel any warmer, or any safer. Only the matches as they sparked to fire near her eyes did that.

* * *

Strike five—last match. Last light. Last warmth. Poor girl's fingers were too frozen by then to be careful, and she caught the edge of the match on the side of her wooden cheeks. By accident? By accident. She went up in flames—poor design!—but she was not unhappy, in those last moments when she was alight, because she forgot about the bird and its broken leg, and the man who cried for ants, and a woman with a broken face in a basement, and she forgot that she was hungry. All that she knew was her face felt so alight! So red! She was the brightest part of the world.

* * *

Her body crumbled to black soot in the snow.

* * *

And so it was that, some time later, a group of revelers on their evening walk came across the black stain of her body with five burnt-out matches beside it. Each felt a quick little agony in their heart as they shaped the black into the body of a girl in their mind. As soon as they did, each one thought, well, this little thing has succumbed to her pain, hasn't she? Animal like, at the end. One by one, they walked away, and did not think of her ever again.

Home Belly Wants

I want a womb. I wonder if mother notices how hungry I am for hers, how I look at her belly, expanded past her hip bones, filled with cakes, cookies, meats dripping with good sauces, upset that those stretch marks are from sugar and fat and not from me. My own body grew and stretched out a foreign woman with familiar skin.

I am jealous of the kids who can point to their mothers and say, this is where my synapses were brought together, strapped and crisscrossed in pink. Electrified. Or this is the place where my body-cord pulsed with blood, was connected to the source. Where is my source? To what ash have I sprung, and to what dust shall I return? I am homeless in a home.

In bright and cold September mother comes into the basement where I sleep, cocooned by the darkness of bulbs that have never been replaced. Her voice is soft. She says my name. She says my name again. "Are you awake? The doctor called. It's diseased from disuse. They have to cut it out. Are you awake?"

We sit, together, on an old rocking chair that was my grandmother's. Though I am grown, I curl up on her lap and put my hands on her, whispering healing nonsense. I get down on my knees and kiss her swollen belly.

They cut it out. I wonder, after they sliced and diced, if they held it in their hands like something precious. Was it deflated, rubbery, bloody skin ripped apart? Or was it golden, like the ball the princess dropped, a treasure hidden so deep in my mother's body she forgot it was there yet, like all treasures, has a way of being discovered?

When she is healed, we spend our evenings on her bed. Her belly is misshapen. There is an indentation where parts used to be.

"Come here," she says. "Look, they made room for you."

The space is big enough for my head. It is comfortable. My face makes an outline in her skin. Mother wraps her fingers in my hair and holds tight.

Mama floriculture

The seventh child would be perfect. She would make sure of it, just as she made sure her hair was expertly coiffed each morning, and her front and back garden were in bloom when spring came.

The previous six came forth wailing ugly notes and flailing thick, bulbous arms and thighs. They'd been malformed, throwing what should have been cherubic off. The firstborn was inexplicably wretched, covered in blood, like weepy milkweed, and so she had to bury it the moment it detached. But that son had grown lovely orchids above him, the little dear, and so she was not mad at him anymore. And, at least, he told her what to expect with the second. She did not look at that daughter until the girl had been cleaned off and smoothed out, wrapped in a clean towel. But there were indents under her bright blue eyes, thick gashes where the skin met itself, so she too went into the ground and made tea roses that all the neighbor ladies stopped and admired. The third was a funny color, like rotten azaleas, but it had been close to beautiful, so she kept it in a pot against her bedroom window, and was now her tulip child. None of the rest had even come close, and so they were in the earth or in barrels of dirt, their tiny bones growing something more lovely above them.

It saddened her when she realized the imperfection was her own refined body. It was spoiling their pliant flesh before birth. So when the seventh child was seeded months in her belly, she reached inside herself and squeezed the slick, bloody flesh, put too much pressure on her bladder (she wet herself, but it was over the bathtub, and she held her breath until it was all down the drain), pinched his slippery toes between her thumb and forefinger and yanked him out.

She checked the normal things: ten fingers, ten toes, two feet, a torso, and two eyes evenly spaced. He wailed an unfinished voice, so she plugged her ears with wax and hummed La Vie en Rose.

She examined him under glass to see where the rot began, and there it was: his middle finger was a smidge too long. Glaringly wrong, wrong, wrong among the cultivated rest. She used garden shears, rusted from the sinewy threads of last year's annuals, and deadheaded the tip. She kissed the mole near his eye. Pretty boy. Snip.

His finger leaked sappy blood, ugly sticky stuff, but she cooed him without looking, and when he'd calmed she bundled him up in her hands, spread her legs apart and shoved him back inside. Another month's germination and she'd take him out again for another trim. When he came out for the last time, pruned, glorious, cut away to the best whole, he would be everything she could ever hope for, a real blue-ribbon winner of a boy.

Egest Leporidae

The first miscarriage was odd, but not odd enough to cause alarm. The flesh dripped out wrong, in pieces unfamiliar, not human, all pink gummy flesh and blood clots. Her husband only sighed and did the duty of his labor: he buried the meat in the yard under the oak, then took her to bed again.

She told him that she had seen a rabbit that morning, before it went wrong. The rabbit looked at her, its black, little eyes big and round, and she had been afraid.

He told her not to speak of it.

Her belly grew from that night, and after the heavy months passed she went into labor again. Her mother-in-law, who was called in because she was a midwife, and because her husband suspected the first had been mishandled, came into the birth late, and by the time she arrived there was no baby, but skinned parts of lean legs, a purple liver and lungs, and curved ears with long veins.

Her husband fed the pieces to the cat and took her to bed again.

The next birth had him pacing outside her door. When his mother came out with the offering, it was of three long legs with tufts of black fur around its ankles, a long vertebrae with no extensions for arms or legs, and guts winding around the lump.

His wife told them she was dreaming of their cat, which had run away not too long ago, and she thought of it, then, when she was pushing.

Over the next few days, when her husband went to lie with her again, she said she was too ill, and when they woke up there were black eyes and brains between her legs.

At a loss, her husband called in the doctors, who did not believe in such miracles, and they examined the newest parts and said they were too carefully butchered—knife scratches on the bones—and told him to lie with her again. Then, they tied her legs together and tied the rest of her to the bed, only allowing her to sip spoons of vegetable soup. They shuttered the windows, so that she might not see any animals, though she still heard the birds outside, twittering their songs, and at night, the scream of the rabbits as they were butchered for the doctor's meals.

After the months passed, they untied her and pushed on her belly. A skinned young rabbit with broken teeth flushed out under her dress, as well as so much blood. The cord was still attached to it, and when they pulled on it, it came out from under her as if it had been connected to nothing.

Madness, they told one another. It is pure madness.

They bet their degrees on a hoax and informed the husband that he should lie with her one more time. This time, they allowed her to move, but they watched her carefully in shifts so that she was never alone, and kept her diet strictly to cabbage and oil. Against propriety and her wishes, they sat in the corner of the room as she birthed, smoking cigars and rubbing their foreheads.

The rabbit came out alive, twitching and squealing.

"My child," she said to it, and asked it to be placed in her arms.

The mother-in-law made to do so, but the doctors snatched it from her arms and threw it against the wall. Then they fell on her as one, tearing the clothes from her body as the women screamed at them to stop. When the mother was naked and sobbing, they backed away from her. The mother-in-law stepped forward and dared put her hands in the space between her legs to feel the soft, gray fur covering her from thigh to belly.

strange folk

The boys came back from the elm covered in dirt, and they did not come back alone.

Their jeans were a mess. Denim soaked up stains like a dry rag in oil, and there were too many spots to avoid a trip to the laundromat, but one look at the girl's face and any yell Bella may have made withered in her throat. The girl, the stranger, was a young thing, probably the age of the twins, but was the kind of girl who looked one minute older. She was pretty enough, except for her feet dragging mud in the kitchen like a follow-me trail, but her eyes were odd. Off. Open just a bit too wide; there was too much white showing. Bella could not tell if she was afraid or enraged, and her mouth gave no indication either way.

"Mom," Georgie said, tugging Bella's hand. "Can we keep her?" Artie, his twin in all but manners, stared at the ground. He was the smarter of the two, and he knew what Bella would say.

"She doesn't belong to us," Bella said, avoiding the girl's big white eyes. "Go on home now."

For a moment, Bella thought the girl was dumb and deaf because she didn't make any movement to show she heard. She didn't even blink. Just stared for a long moment, long enough to make the guts clench. Then she turned around and left out the kitchen door, like she'd never been there at all, except for her footprints.

Bella didn't know how long she stared after her, but it must have been long enough to make the twins feel awkward. Georgie seized her in a hug meant to penetrate, but a ten-year-old only has so much strength, and she only had eyes for the door, only had feelings for the breeze coming through. Artie moved her arms to wrap around Georgie, and when the boys went to bed there was a wet spot on her dress. Thank goodness, salt from the eyes don't stain. No need to go to the laundromat for that.

* * *

There was an art to gambling how long clothes can hold up before needing to be cleaned. Jeans could go the longest, provided they were the dark kind. Bella had a point system. Fourteen days for jeans, subtract a day for wear, so long as you only normal-sweat. You might go longer in the colder months without too much of the water leaking out of your skin. Shirts were always bought black, because they hide stains the best, but you could get away with a navy blue dress for the rare occasion you can't get out of going to church, though it had been a long time since Bella couldn't get out of going to church. She learned long ago the value a "yeah, maybe" could have in conversation. A bra did not need to be washed until it smelled, and you only had to wear a bra when others were around. The big problem was underwear, and the hole between her legs. She took to wearing dresses whenever she could and went without panties, and if she did have to go to town a carefully folded wad of toilet paper caught most of the drippings. It meant a longer reprieve from washers and dryers.

No matter how perfected her art, though, the boys had a way of making her go earlier than her system allowed. At least they were old enough to leave at home when she went to town—two less things to worry about—though unsupervised they were likely to go and get their clothes soaked in mud and grease. It was an endless, useless battle, like that man Bella heard about in school who was pushing a rounded stone up a mountain. She didn't understand it at the time why he didn't let the rock roll to the bottom and give up, but as she grew she figured the rock wasn't just a rock, but all sorts of detergents and softeners.

She made the boys peanut butter sandwiches—two each, loaded with cream until it was likely to burst out the edges with a good squeeze—in the hopes that while she was away they would rub their bellies and take an afternoon nap. The laundry took up most of the backseat of her little gray two-door and piled up so she could barely see out the top of the rear window, but there was no need to look behind.

In the parking lot, she loitered, car still running, until Martha Gladsby noticed her through the large, smudged windows of the laundromat. Martha, at eighty-three years old, kept working because her son thought if she got out of the house she would live a more fulfilling life, but he didn't know that she had a nicotine addiction as strong as her affection for yelling at teenagers. Because she had lied to him for years about quitting, she needed to get away from him every day to sneak the long, thin sticks she was fond of. Everyone in the town who didn't have their own washer and dryer had an agreement of some kind with Martha: you didn't snitch on her to her son, and she didn't say anything if you washed underwear that didn't belong to your spouse. Bella and Martha had a different agreement; Martha gave her a nod if it was safe to enter, and Bella explained to Martha's son that the yellow stains on his mother's fingers were from the chemicals in the soaps, nothing more.

"He was here earlier this week," Martha said as Bella walked in with her first load. "Doubt he'll be back today."

Bella nodded and filled one machine before going back to her car for another load.

"Were you in town yesterday?" Martha asked her once Bella had five machines running. "No, I suppose not. Leaves are changing. The tourists are upon us." Martha rolled her eyes all the way around her sockets. They both shared the same opinion on their annual visitors.

Martha continued to prattle at her. At her age, the old woman no longer required the help of another conversationalist to keep the chatter going, though she did appreciate a body in clear view. Bella sat curled on the floor next to the machines, counting the rhythmic bumping. She no longer needed to wait for the ding to know when it was done. She had a system for this, too.

"...and goodness knows they don't watch their children," Martha said over the dull hum of the machine. She repeated this line again, and again, until Bella lost count of the rhythm and looked out the window where the old woman was pointing a yellowed finger.

It was that girl from the night before. She wore the same graying dress that fell just a little bit below her knees and no shoes, even though she was standing on cracked concrete. There was no expression on her face, save those too-large, too-white eyes, open as wide as human skin is allowed to stretch. The girl was staring straight at Bella, and Bella could do nothing but stare back at her and concentrate on her own breathing.

Remember, one breath in, one breath out, focus on the way it enters and exits your body. Everything that enters your body will eventually leave. One in, one out.

The ding of the dryer startled Bella into a cry, and she got to her feet out of habit. When she looked out the window again, the girl had turned around and was walking away on her dirty feet.

Martha shivered and reached under her chair where she kept a packet of cigarettes duct taped. "Ugh," she said. "I feel like someone walked on my grave."

* * *

Over a decade ago, a young man who believed himself to be a small-town poet took to writing verse in his head at the coffee shop and the courthouse, but found the ambient noise to be all a little too much for slant rhymes. He decided he was a nature poet, a poet of the plains, and instead took long walks through the fields and sparse trees. One day, as he was leaning against a large, rotting elm tree on a small hill, thinking of what he could say about dead wood in spring, he felt a sharp pain in his back. Examining the tree closely, there was an odd white lump, barely visible. He tore away at the wood and found, to his horror and delight, a skull peeking back at him, with fungus veined out around the left eye socket. He did the appropriate thing, which to him was to alert the local authorities, but also the local paper. A reporter caught the photos of her whole skeleton as it was dislodged from the body of the tree, almost like she had been consummated and grown there.

The whole thing became something of a small sensation, enough where folks who wouldn't have dared taken their town exit before now made a short detour to see the tree-woman with her fungus face, and bits of taffeta lodged in her throat, kept on display at town hall after no one claimed the body. It was gruesome, the town agreed, but it was hard to argue with the influx of tourists and tourist wallets. Even the tree was left in as much peace as it could be, though it was torn in half and worms had taken up residence there, eating and defecating in a cycle of mud.

Bella only made two trips to the tree in her life, and only one to see the skull. As a child, her father decided he ought to know what the whole hullabaloo was and took her to the tree first. "It's a tree," he said, all disappointment, even though there was a small plaque commemorating the woman. Not much was known about her, the sign said, but more than likely she'd been in the tree for fifty years, based on the fungus growth, and, of course, someone had put her there. Dutifully, her father followed the suggestion at the bottom of the plaque, which was to take the three mile walk to town, and he held Bella up by her armpits so she could get a better look at the display.

She didn't remember much about the trip, but her father always reminded her how she screamed something fierce when she saw the skull.

They never did find out who murdered the woman in the tree, or who she was. The mystery only added to the income. All sorts of amateur sleuths ate the story and their fill of burgers with American cheese at the local grill and bar. The mayor named the exhibit "Strange Folk," and used tax dollars to fund billboards on the side of the highway three miles in each direction. "Come visit the Strange Folk," they said beside a painted skull.

* * *

The sandwich trick worked, thank goodness. Both boys were yawning away the nap from their faces when she returned and dumped piles of clean clothes on her bed. In order to get out of the laundromat sooner, Bella didn't bother folding the clothes at the machines. The boys started separating clothes into their own piles to bring to their bedroom, aimlessly bickering over whose shirt was whose, even though most of them were solid black and the same size.

That evening, the boys were uncharacteristically quiet. Usually, they were loud and screaming at one another. They were still working out the benefits of sharing, and Bella could rarely afford two of the same toy at once. They sat on the battered couch from the local thrift store and whispered, shooting looks at their mother when they thought she wasn't looking. She was looking—at ten years old, they were too young to be subtle or secretive—but she graciously allowed them the illusion of privacy. Her habit, at the end of a day, was to sit near the little window in her living room on her grandfather's rocking chair and sway back and forth, forward and back, until the boys decided it was time to turn their minds to dream. Her window faced the hill with the tree, but in the darkness, at that distance, Bella imagined there was no tree on the hill, no skull in the courthouse, no body on the grass. She only imagined a long stretch of emptiness, expanding out like the unfurling of a great winged animal, all that soft black, punctured with small dots of white.

The boys stopped whispering to one another and looked out into the darkness, but Bella could not see what grasped their attention. Georgie took to his feet and ran out into the field, clumsily slipping, more than likely staining his jeans with green and brown, but Bella did nothing more than stop her rocking. How far could he go in the darkness? And, anyway, his brother would bring him back if he wandered too far.

Soon enough he returned and he did not return alone. He dragged that pale, strange girl behind him, like an overexcited dog tugging on the leash. Artie ran to meet them partway across the lawn, and the boys began to argue, raising their voices loud enough for Bella to know they were upset, but not loud enough for her to make out what they were saying. The girl stared in the window, directly at Bella. Neither of them blinked.

There was not much hope that ignoring the issue would make it fade into memory, so Bella rose from her chair and went outside.

"She can't stay out here all night," Georgie said as soon as he spotted Bella. "It's cold," he added, as if Bella was unaware of the temperature.

Artie stared at her, face blank, except for the wrinkles near his eyes.

"Where is your family?" Bella asked the girl.

The girl did not open her mouth, and Bella wondered what the girl was keeping closed up inside of her. Was that the reason she did not speak? She never believed the stories, but her parents were often fond of telling each other fairy tales of girls and boys who coughed up frogs and toads when too much rain threatened to drown the harvest. Horrible stories. Even though her parents told her—it's made up! Imagine all those slimy things swimming around the wet land, having the time of their lives—Bella kept her mouth clamped shut for almost a month, only drinking water through a straw, and was only relieved from the fear of monsters swimming around in her belly, waiting to be released, when her mother washed her mouth out with soap, telling her the bubbles would drown anything alive down there.

"She can stay the night with us," Artie finally said, as if he had the authority to make such decisions. "We'd be bad if we didn't let her."

The girl's wide eyes were too awful to look at, so damned white. Bella turned away from the three children and walked back into the house, which her sons took as permission, and dragged the girl along with them, each of them taking an arm and pulling.

Inside, as they released her, the boys marveled at how where they'd touched her they'd left black marks on her skin and checked their own palms to see if they were dirty.

Georgie rushed to his own bed and started to pull out sheets to make up the couch for the girl, and though Bella couldn't bear the thought of the girl's dirty feet on anything that needed to be washed immediately, she said nothing. She waved at the girl to follow her and ran the hot water in the tub.

"Water's hot," Bella remembered to say.

The girl could borrow Georgie's t-shirt and shorts—they looked to be about the same size. Bella told her to leave her dusty dress on the tile. The girl grasped the ends of her dress and lifted it above her head. Bella looked away and made her exit, but not before noticing that the girl wore nothing underneath.

She closed the door so the boys wouldn't see and waited until she heard the sounds of water splashing before heading to the linen closet for a towel. She paused and sniffed the extra one they had for spills. She'd done it with the load that day and didn't fancy having someone else's sweat on it. Bella went into the kitchen and gathered a load of rags, mostly ripped from clothes she no longer fit into, and thought they'd have to do.

As the boys prepared the couch, Bella knocked on the bathroom door and asked if she could come in to drop off the rags and some clean clothes. There was no response, so Bella pressed her ear against the door. She heard nothing, and imagined, for a moment, that the girl had drowned. That would be a right mess, wouldn't it? There would be all sorts of people in her home, then. Policemen, a coroner, perhaps even a priest to talk to the boys about the cycles of life, and none of them were likely to wipe their feet at the door or remove their shoes. Plus, it would upset the boys, and they were the type who got into trouble when they were upset.

She turned the knob on the bathroom door and went in and was surprised to see that the girl had not closed the shower curtain, but was sitting in the tub with her knees raised to her chin and her arms wrapped around herself.

"There's soap," Bella said, in an attempt to encourage the girl to wash her skin. "Dry off when you're done." She dropped the rags at the edge of the sink.

The girl looked at her, eyes so wide and white.

And then, she frowned.

Her lips were pale and thin, and that slight downturn made her whole face into something ugly, something that made Bella wish she herself had eyelids as thick as iron, something strong enough to block out that face, but even as she closed the flesh around her eyes, she still saw the girl, still saw her staring like she could stare right into the center of any living thing and find something wrong.

Bella retreated into her room and went under the covers, something she rarely did to avoid washing the sheets. She curled into a ball and made sure not even a lick of her hair was sticking out from underneath. Can't hurt you if you can't see 'em.

* * *

Bella did not sleep well. Years of practice had taught her the value of not letting her mind wander, not during the day, and certainly not at night when there was no light to distract her. Her mother once told her a wandering mind will inevitably find a trail of sweets, but the more you eat, the more you follow, and eventually you'll find an oven at the end of it, and a witch with sick-black teeth and one outstretched palm. Bella always thought those stories were dumb, but she took the advice to heart.

She tried, anyway. She closed her eyes, tensed her limbs, and thought about that tree, lonesome on the hill, how it never really left her mind, but sat near the edge of her memory like a soldier, ready always with a rifle, ready always to aim, ready always to explode.

She knew a secret, though. The town fell over themselves with the easy questions—how could a body be so broken to end up in the hollow? None of those found bones were bent, and yet she fit into a space no human should be allowed to. Bella knew. Her own body had twisted and bent like a bow, like a reed in the air, and it had become as small and motionless as a baked pretzel, left on the grass, all that soiling green. Those stains didn't come out. She had to throw out the blue dress she'd worn. How cruel that grass had been. Why hadn't it washed out? She should have used lye.

Bella emerged her head from the covers to take a breath of cool air. The girl was there, at the foot of her bed, staring, staring, staring. Bella did not scream. She'd long ago kept that noise buried in her lungs to rot, but she did inhale, in and out, in and out.

"Go to bed," she said, because that worked on her sons. The girl did not blink, did not twist her face, but she raised her hand and pointed her finger at Bella's head, like an accusation.

"I said," Bella repeated, "go to bed."

The girl turned around and drifted out, and Bella stared after her for a long while, then went back under the covers.

There was something terribly wrong with that girl. It was as if she had seen a ghost.

* * *

The boys argued that they should accompany their new friend to town and Bella only put up a minor protest. In truth, she didn't want to be alone in the car with the girl.

Because Bella was practical, she loaded up the trunk with the sheets the boys used for a makeshift bed and added the comforters off of their twin beds. Comforters took too long, you had to dry them at least twice, and she did not remember the last time she had them cleaned. She could drop Georgie off at the laundromat to keep an eye on the load. Martha could be trusted to keep him in line. The old woman couldn't keep her eye on both of them, but Georgie shrank when anyone raised their voice to him, and Martha enjoyed the high cadence she could reach. She handed Artie a scribbled grocery list of nonperishable foods—pastas, mostly, and jars of peanut butter and tomato sauce. The sorts of things you could stock up on. Because they were inclined to whine that their new acquaintance was going bye-bye, she added honey to the list for them to spoon into their mouths. Sweetness to cover their inevitable sour moods.

Bella must have sucked up all the uneasiness into her own belly, because the boys shared none of it. The three of them sat in the back, the boys on either side of the girl, which unfortunately meant that anytime Bella looked in the rear-view mirror, she would see those eyes.

Thankfully, there was no reason to look behind.

Georgie asked the girl all sorts of questions—where was she from? Did she like winter better than summer? What was her favorite color? Has she ever seen a dragonfly? Why didn't she like to wear shoes? Did she also think the sky was too big sometimes? That the girl didn't answer, or even acknowledge him, didn't seem to bother him, but he'd asked those questions of Bella before, and got a similar response. Perhaps he was used to it.

Artie took the girl's hand and splayed his fingers across hers, holding them up to his face.

"We match," he said, all wonder. "We're the same size."

"Leave her alone," Bella said, though she didn't know why she said it.

* * *

Martha frowned at the girl in the back of the car, but she dutifully took Georgie by the hand and lead him to the machines. She gave him a lollipop when he started asking her if she liked ducks. She did, she told him, but not enough to carry a whole conversation about it.

"There's something wrong with that girl," Martha said. "Makes my whole throat dry."

Bella wanted to say the cigarettes were the likely cause, but she only nodded her agreement.

"Something familiar looking about her," Martha added, tapping her cheek. "But she's too pale to be from around here. Goodness, her skin looks like it's paper. Think someone's kept her locked up in a cupboard?"

"I don't know," Bella said. And she wasn't about to find out. Other people's pain was just that—belonging to them, and none of her business.

* * *

After dropping off Artie at the store with a wad of singles and fives, she drove to city hall, and the skull. She wasn't sure where you dropped off unwanted, lost children, but she suspected the people who collected taxes would have some idea.

It was impossible to avoid the skull, not in a place that collected little agonies. There were smaller displays littered in the center of town hall, some perhaps real, and others very clearly made up from bored, sick minds. Discovering that woman in the tree gave them the right to collect and display all manner of local atrocities, like they were immune to horror now, and could collect a few more pieces. To the left, a pile of poorly woven cloth from a girl who once lost a weaving contest, which is one of the worst things you can do, if you are a girl. Lose. She hung herself, in her grief, because no one ever let her forget that one time she had not won, that time her fingers slipped the loop, that time she meant to use black thread, but instead had brought so much white. She died doing what she loved, tying strings together around her neck, and knotting them to the rafters above her bed. All those people who made her feel small? They felt bad, too, in that way that grief curls into your throat tight enough to make you choke on it if you inhale too fast. So they undid her last knot and put her body in the ground to nourish the spiders, all those spinning small things. Perhaps they hoped the creatures would spin her out anew, make of her flesh into silk, so they wouldn't feel so bad anymore.

There was a helpful little sign under the display: Remember to be happy.

To the right, a lump of what was more than likely coal dusted with green and brown paint, but was said to have come from the local reservoir—the fossilized remains of a monster, under consideration for study from the local university's anthropology department.

Above them hung a wooden flute that was said to produce the most beautiful music in the world, but only people who had died could hear it, so it was floating above them, like a reminder that there was beautiful music in heaven. You'd hear it eventually, if you were good enough.

There, a shrunken head, and over there, golden coins that almost certainly did not have chocolate inside. Different administrations put more effort into the collection than others.

But the main attraction was the first.

Once Bella and the girl entered the building there were printed banners announcing its presence, along with viewing hours, guided tours that lead tourists to the tree and back to the skull again, ending with a meal at the diner, which had become adept at making skull shaped pancakes. There was a garishness to this presentation of pain that made Bella almost apologize to the girl for forcing her to look at it, but she didn't want to say anything. She never really wanted to say anything.

As Bella attempted to read the directory and figure out where it was best to take her—would the Lost and Found work? It was technically correct—the girl walked towards the skull, as if possessed.

Not wanting to lose her before she got rid of her, Bella trailed after.

The skull was like she remembered, but also unlike she remembered. In her memory, it was larger, and the vein-like fungus near the eye socket pulsated as if blood was running through it. The teeth were smaller than she recalled, but larger than the ones in her own mouth. They looked like a row of weapons. Whoever this woman was, once upon a time, she must have had very thick lips to fully hide those fangs.

Bella wondered if the girl, too, had a row of weapons in her mouth, but the girl's lips were so pale it was impossible to tell where the smoothness of her cheeks ended and the stitch of those lips began. The girl was frowning, again, in that ugly way of hers, but she was not frowning at the skull, no, she was frowning through the glass at a tall man walking out of the elevator.

Breathe in, breathe out.

He had not grown much since she had seen him full on, not just a glance through the laundromat window before turning around, not since that night in her blue dress, the one that her mother made for her and made her look like a prairie princess. She'd twirled in front of her mirror for hours, just to see the cotton move. She no longer had the dress, but he still sported close cropped hair and a severe line of bangs at the edge of his forehead. She'd called his hair silly that night. He didn't listen to her then, and it seemed he hadn't listened since.

He saw her.

It was inevitable. Nothing that is buried can stay in the ground. All sorts of things will bring it to the surface. Worms and germs. It all turns to worms and germs eventually.

He walked towards her. Bella did not move. That's the sort of thing animals did when they were afraid, freeze or flee, and Bella was not the type of woman who really learned the value of running. Not until it was much, much later.

But he, too, froze, and Bella wondered, for a hysterical moment, if she had made him do that, if her face showed how much she didn't want him near her, and if he learned how to read her after all, but he did not look at her. He looked at the girl.

Bella held her breath, the same way one does when they are driving past a cemetery, lest you be the one buried next, and backed away. One step under and over the next—there's no need to look behind you. She felt the door behind her, reached for the knob, opened it and turned, running out into the sun, but not before seeing the girl raise her finger to point at him.

* * *

Even before the body was found crammed inside, the elm tree had been an unsettling site. Most trees grew reaching towards the sky, with long, thick branches peppered with leaves. This tree grew squat and fat, out instead of up, and the branches grew out at angles this direction and that, so it resembled an angry porcupine. Bella's second trip to the tree was on a bet, the kind with no physical stakes but loads of social ones.

He was the one who asked her there, him and a group of his friends, boys and girls, not the most popular or good looking group, but the kind who were respectful to adults and sometimes able to snatch a small bottle of gin from one of their parents for sharing. He complimented her dress, said she looked nice in the way only a young boy can make such a mundane compliment sound like he was head over heels.

They sat on a blanket in front of the tree as if they were all about to have a picnic, but they only had alcohol, and dared one another to go inside the tree. The girls, including Bella, blanched at the thought, but he smiled at her and asked her if she was a newborn chicken with all the fluff between her ears, and so, after a boy or two tried and failed (too big, their growing bodies) to go in and said there weren't any worms (they were lying), Bella got up, folded her body, and went into the husk.

* * *

Martha asked if something was wrong when Bella came back to pick up Georgie, but Bella took the boy by his hand and dragged him into the back of the car where Artie was trying, unsuccessfully, to unscrew the honey jar.

"Where's our friend?" Georgie asked. "Did you find her family?"

Bella slammed the door on him and got behind the wheel. She peeled out of the parking lot so fast she almost hit Martha, who was waving a rag from the pile Bella forgot about.

No time, no time, don't look behind.

* * *

Georgie pressed himself against her on the couch and intertwined his fingers with her palm, telling her that one day, his hand would be bigger than hers.

Bella allowed him to twist her hand and arm this way and that. She concentrated on her breathing. She took the plate Artie gave her—honey and peanut butter with white bread—but kept it in her lap until Georgie asked her for a bite. The boys asked her if they could watch television and took her lack of a response as permission. Artie sat on the other end of the couch, away from her, but he looked at her from the corner of his eye.

Georgie fell asleep with his head on her lap, and Artie moved her arm so it would rest on his brother's shoulder. It was late enough where the only thing playing on the few stations they got was infomercials, but neither Bella nor Artie moved to change the channel. He opened and closed his mouth a few times, huffing out breath at the beginning of sentences he never finished.

He gave up on trying and looked out the window instead. Bella closed her eyes and concentrated on the feel of her eyelids pressed together.

"Mom," Artie said.

Bella was not sleeping, but she did not open her eyes either.

"Mom, wake up."

He'd said this to her before, on those occasional days when she stayed on top of her bed well past the lunch hour, and she gave him the same response she did then.

"Georgie," Artie said, shaking his brother. "She's back."

Bella did open her eyes then. The girl was outside their window, staring in at them, eyes so white, so wide.

Bella sucked in the air through her teeth.

* * *

"You oughta be locked up, the way you drive," Martha cheerfully said over Bella's small kitchen table. She came bearing gifts for the family—two bright lollipops for the boys and Bella's forgotten laundry. When she saw the girl, she apologized for not having the foresight to bring three lollipops, but the girl only stared at her until the boys lead her out into the yard to play with a half deflated basketball.

"I'm being haunted," Bella said.

"That's no excuse for almost hitting people with your car," Martha joked, but she turned her eyes to where the children were playing. The girl sat on the lawn while the boys threw the ball with increasing intensity at one another, all while looking back at the girl to make sure she was watching when they caught it.

"She keeps coming back," Bella said.

"I thought you dropped her off with the authorities yesterday," Martha said, eyeing Bella's teapot. "Do you mind if I make myself a cup?"

"I…" Bella said. "He was there."

Martha frowned and patted Bella on the shoulder. "Let me make you a cup of tea. Where do you keep it?"

Bella pointed to the top of the fridge and Martha busied herself with filling the teapot under the faucet.

"Some things," Martha said, slowly, tasting each word in her mouth like it was a lemon, "are inevitable. Take my cigarettes, for example. I know each day is closer to the one where I won't be able to breathe."

Bella looked at her.

"Goodness," said Martha, "your stove is old." She turned the knob. "Like I was saying, some things are inevitable. You're bound to run into him eventually. No matter how many precautions you take."

"She keeps coming back," Bella said.

"So you said," Martha replied.

"I think," Bella said, tasting the words on her tongue and finding them sour, "I think she's a ghost."

Martha hummed. "I thought ghosts were invisible."

Bella blinked. "I…"

As the water heated up, Martha brought up all other sorts of facts she knew about ghosts: they were often tied to places, not people, they could be malevolent, not just irritating, and they were stuck between two places they could not reach, life and the afterlife, so it was a little unreasonable to expect a girl whose feet were getting dirty and who everyone could plainly see was anything other than that. Plus, ghosts did things like move furniture or flicker lights. They didn't just stare at people.

"Where did you learn all that?" Bella asked as the teapot screamed.

"The tours. They're claiming the motel is haunted now. Lets them charge ten extra a night."

Bella took the cup of tea Martha offered and sipped. It burned and tasted cheap, but it was the kind of cheap burn Bella was used to. She didn't want to say any more, but this was a rare opportunity to talk to someone. Her sons wouldn't understand. They were too young. Even mad words need to be voiced, sometimes.

"I went into the tree," Bella said.

Martha tsked and blew on her drink. "Recently?"

"No, no. Before the boys. When he…I don't believe in this sort of thing. But that woman was murdered and put there and I disturbed her…her grave."

Martha cut her off. "I hardly think a ghost would wait that long to begin haunting you. Isn't there a time limit for that sort of thing?"

"What else could it be?" Bella asked.

Martha sighed and muttered something about Bella talking to someone, specifically someone who was not Martha, about this, but she sipped her tea and threaded her fingers on the table. "If this is true, and I don't want to give fanciful ideas any weight, but if it was, I think removing her bones from the wood would have been more disturbing than a teenage girl going inside. You think you're the first one who ever did that?"

"No, but—"

"But nothing. She's odd, I'll grant you that. Lord, she's looking at us right now." Martha frowned at the window. Bella didn't look. "She's lost and she's attached herself to you. Her parents are probably worried sick about her."

Bella rubbed her temples.

"You know, it's funny. I think this is the most you've ever said to me. She's really got you bothered, doesn't she? Look," Martha said gently, "I came for two reasons today. Your laundry and because he came into the store last night. Asking after you, like when you usually came in. He said he wanted to talk to you."

Bella placed her hands in her lap and looked out the window at the girl. The boys were still throwing the ball at one another, but the girl was looking in at Bella, that frown dipping her face ugly.

"I said it was none of my business," Martha continued on. "But he's a tenacious one."

* * *

Wearing one of Artie or Georgie's shirts, the girl, somehow, managed to look even more pale with the black against her skin. She didn't answer any of Georgie's questions, and though Bella had a few of her own, she figured if the girl didn't want to talk to him, she probably wasn't going to talk to her either. She didn't eat or drink anything, even though Artie insisted that Bella make her a sandwich. Either she didn't like well water or, as Bella was now convinced, the girl wasn't from this world.

The boys watched television that evening and Bella excused herself to sit on the porch. She assumed the girl would follow her and she didn't want the boys to hear.

After some time, the girl did follow her out. She stood until Bella asked her to sit next to her, and was surprised to see the girl listened, crossing her legs over one another, the same way her boys sat. Bella looked at the girl's belly, trying to see if there was the slow up and down of breathing, but the shirt was too baggy on her.

"Why," Bella started, almost losing her nerve. The girl turned to face her. "Why are you here?"

She didn't know what she expected the girl to do: open her mouth and say, "I'm from Pittsburgh and I got lost?" or "You disturbed my favorite worm that day, and it took me over ten years to find you." This close, Bella could see the green speckled in the girl's brown irises, a really pretty color, like her mother had when she still had eyes, and would have suited the girl's face fine if her eyes weren't so damn big.

"Are you haunting me?" Bella finally asked. The girl did not respond, but her eyes, somehow, beyond the limits of the possible, got even larger.

All the unsettling feelings, guts churned, teeth rubbed against the enamel of each other, the part where you can feel your skin covering you, holding you in, the moment when you are aware of your mouth taking in air, rolling into your lungs and releasing, overcame Bella, and she was almost knocked sideways by the whole of it, all at once.

It had been a long time since she felt much, except fear, except smallness.

She thought about all the comforting things in the world; how linen smelled like clean when it came out of the dryer, how the knobs ticked over each setting, how socks can be turned inside out to give them a few more wears, how nice it was to not smell like a body on that day after the laundry was done, how she was never reminded that she had a body on those days, before the sweat set in. How it bought her time between the risk of the next clean. But even those things could not make her forget what her body felt like, what her voice sounded like in her head, as one does after they awaken from a deep slumber, and memory drives forward to awareness.

Awakened.

"Where did you come from?" Bella asked, the words pulled out of her lips.

The girl turned her head to the distance, out towards the fields where, a few miles away, the tree sat alone on a small hill, and pointed.

* * *

The air smelled bad in the tree, like sour wine and dirt. It had been reconstructed as best as possible after the bones were removed, so little light managed to penetrate inside. Bella had to duck and twist herself to get her whole body to fit, and her nose touched the wood when she was fully confined. She held her breath as long as possible, straining to hear the cheers of the others outside the wood. The longer she stayed inside, the longer they would admire her, but she could only hold her breath for a little over a minute, and when she released it she tasted the air and almost blanched, and felt something crawl on her arm, wet and sick.

She heard herself screaming and she did not stop until he reached inside and pulled her out.

"It's okay," he hold her as he gathered her in his arms. "It's alright. It's just a tree."

The others were looking at her with a mix of amusement and disgust. One of them called her a pussy.

"Go off," he told them. "None of you had the guts to go in."

He held her as she shook and rubbed at her arms, trying to get rid of the feeling of that small, living thing on her. He held her even as the others left, bored with the tree or with her, and then she started to cry. She couldn't help herself.

"Hey, hey now," he said. "It's okay. Just look forward, okay? Look at all that green. Don't look behind you. You won't see it if you look straight ahead. If you don't see it, it's not there, right?"

Right. She looked ahead, out into the expanse of green and browning grass, and thought it was good advice.

Such good advice, she kept looking ahead when he put his cheek against hers and repeated, don't look behind you. She didn't look behind her when he put his lips on her cheek, and didn't move when his hand reached under the neckline of her dirty dress. She didn't look behind her when he dirtied his own clothes by tossing them off, one piece after another, onto the ground.

When he left, when he finally left, Bella breathed in and out, but she did not turn to look at the tree.

* * *

In the morning, she woke up alone, but she woke up feeling. She stood up and felt all the points and pricks that she remembered as numbness fading away from having your arms or legs in one position for too long, and she felt it all over. The light from the sun was too bright, and when she looked out her window at the green grass, the color felt overwhelming.

But it also felt good, like tonguing the sore spot in your gums where the milk teeth were about to come loose.

Artie eyed her with the indignant suspicion only a ten-year-old is capable of. Bella bustled around her little-used kitchen, marveling at just how many wooden spoons she owned as she whipped the children up a batch of cornmeal pancakes after smelling the package to make sure it had not gone bad. She didn't remember when she purchased it. As she whisked the batter she answered Georgie's questions as soon as she could get a word in, though his enthusiasm did not allow her to answer much beyond a yes, no, or I'm not sure before he launched into another set. The girl sat between the boys and watched Bella, but her eyes seemed a little less large this morning, a little less terrifying.

"What do you think her name is?" Georgie asked, kicking his feet back and forth.

"I don't know."

"Everyone has a name."

"Yes."

"I like my name," Georgie said, sniffing the air as the batter hit the oiled pan.

Bella didn't remember who taught her this recipe, but she did remember the movement of flipping the cakes over once the edges were brown. She remembered the smell. It reminded her of Sunday mornings.

She made enough cakes for all of them, and even set a small stack in front of the girl. What was left of the honey was poured on top, and she answered Georgie that, yes, she liked these cakes. Yes, she might make them again tomorrow. Yes, maybe they could have them for dinner, too.

"Can we play outside?" Georgie asked her. The question surprised her; the boys rarely asked her if they could. They often just did.

Bella took a long sip of tea; her throat felt dry from speaking. "I'm taking her back," she told them.

"Back where?" Artie asked, frowning.

"Where she came from."

"Aw," Georgie said. "Where did she come from?" He turned to the girl. "Where did you come from?" Then he looked up at the ceiling and squinted his eyes. "Where did I come from?"

Georgie yelped and glared at his brother. Artie must have kicked him under the table.

After they were done eating the boys piled the plates in the sink. Georgie took the girl to watch cartoons with him with the desperation of someone who is about to lose their beloved pet goldfish. Bella ran the water and poured soap on a sponge that had seen fresher days. She hummed a song that wasn't a song, just noise, deciding that she liked the sound of it all the same.

"Mom?" Artie asked. She turned and looked at him, his scrunched face, the way he twitched his fingers into a fist and back flat again. He took an unsteady step towards her, wobbling in his socks, then slowly put his arms around her waist and burrowed his face into her belly.

"You have to put your arms around me," he said when she didn't move.

"Oh," Bella said, and did.

He felt small and greasy, like all little boys did, but Bella found that she liked the way her fingers felt in his hair, how it reminded her of her own. He left a wet stain on her dress where his face was pressed up against her belly, and Bella thought about how tall he had become.

* * *

There are some stories that say all the pain in the world began at a tree.

From her house it was about a twenty-minute walk, mostly along an old winding two-lane highway. The girl dutifully strayed behind her and waited patiently when Bella slipped over a small hole and fell to her knees, smudging the hem of her dress with dirt. She got up and wiped the mud off her knee where it mixed with a little bit of blood from a scratch. If there was pain, she did not feel it. She thought about how she'd have to wash the dress, how it might need two cycles if the blood set. Not that blood ever really gets out.

The girl's eyes went wide again, and Bella felt the sting in her knees. The pain was a memory of skinned knees and curled toes, and it, inexplicably, as pain can do, helped her put one foot in front of the other.

Cars passed them on the road, going at least ten miles over the already generous speed limit. Someone honked at her and started to slow, but Bella did not turn her head to look. She headed up the small mound, not quite a hill, the girl trailing behind.

In front of the tree, Bella wondered if she miscalculated the journey, though she was so good at futile counting. The tree was smaller than she recalled—in her head, its spindly branches could almost reach the moon, but in the light, with her eyes, it was only a foot or two larger than she was, just a bit squatter than she was, though it was as dark and rotten as she recalled. She waved a limp hand at the tree, a way of saying "well, you're home now," to the girl, but the little thing only stared at her, as if waiting for some miracle.

Bella counted to ten. Then she counted to twenty. Nothing. She thought, perhaps if she counted to the number it takes to finish a load, something would happen. It was a ritual she needed to keep herself quiet, and the girl, if she was from the tree, would need a similar sort of incantation.

"One," Bella started. "Two."

She was halfway to the 1,920 seconds she needed to count when she gave up, seeing as the girl wasn't even moving. At a loss, Bella walked to the sign in front of the tree and read.

No-name woman. Petite. Found with her legs bent into her spine and mushrooms on her face. Snugly-packed, as if she had been born inside. Worms, mud and rot. Perpetrator unknown. To learn more, follow the road to…

"Did it hurt?" Bella asked the girl. "When you were put inside?"

The girl nodded.

Coming up the other side of the hill, she heard the soft stomp of feet moving towards them, and she cursed under her breath that there would be a tour, now, when she was attempting something like an exorcism. But it was not a tour, only a lone man in leather loafers and a crisp button-up, not so different from what he wore that day. Him.

He said her name.

She saw his mouth move, saw how his lips carefully rounded and flattened, how his tongue rested against his front teeth as he tasted letters, but she could not make out what he was saying. She heard only her own smallness, though she was no longer small, how it sounded like the low whine of a teapot on the stove. He moved towards her, raising his hands with his palms out like one does with a frightened stray dog.

"Bella," he said. "There's something I need to say to you."

That, she heard, and opened her mouth to reply, but only a low whine came out.

"Those boys," he kept going. "Are they…?"

She curled down into herself, a ball of flesh and cotton, and put her fingers over her face, but dared not cover her eyes in case he tried to reach out to her.

He stopped, blessedly stopped moving, face scrunched into involuntary disgust. "I'm not trying to scare you," he said. Her fingers shook on her face.

He shook his head and looked around, raising an eyebrow at the girl, then turning his attention back to the huddled woman in front of him. "Okay, okay. How about…how about you go first. Is there anything you want to say to me?"

She opened her mouth, for there were things, buried words, she wished to articulate, but they circled in her lungs and refused to reach her throat, and when she tried to push them out only a gurgle of spit came forward.

He took a step towards her, hand reaching out, and then the girl moved to stand in front of him. He withdrew his hand, his own eyes going wide.

Then, the girl opened her mouth.

Worms and fungus did not fall out of her; instead, it was Bella's own voice, one she recognized from the times when she liked to speak, how she used to like to speak, and she was screaming.

"FIFTEEN MINUTES TO WASH MUD OUT OF BLUE COTTON. TWENTY FOR BLOOD THAT NEVER GETS OUT. THIRTY MINUTES TO DRY. THE BLEACH WILL STAIN. ALL THAT IS LEFT BEHIND ARE STREAKS. CANNOT COLOR THEM IN. IT REMAINS. IT REMAINS. EVERYTHING RUINED REMAINS."

She yelled the brands of Bella's favorite detergent. She screamed how legs hurt to bend. She cried out about the thin layers of panties, and how they cannot catch everything that falls. She yelled how much bleach cost ten years ago when bought in bulk.

Bella closed her eyes under the onslaught of her own voice, and felt herself calm with each shrieked word, as if it was a lullaby, one of those sweet songs she never sang to her boys, or to herself.

When she opened her eyes, the man was gone, as if he had never been there at all. The girl stood before her, her mouth closed and her eyes a little less wide, almost normal for a girl her age, almost like Bella's own.

Bella lifted her hands to the girl, whose own smaller hands met hers. Are these my hands, or hers? But it didn't matter, not really, in that place where hurt was crafted and conceived. There was mud on the tips of the girl's fingers, and Bella bent her head low to put her lips on those stains.

"Come," she told the girl. "Your brothers will want dinner."

They walked off, dirty hand in clean. Before the tree was out of sight, Bella paused to turn around and look at it.

A Girl Without Arms

When she asked about her grandmother, her father lowered his voice and told her the woman was a witch, made of woman's cruel magic—poisons and childbirth. When she lived among people, the villagers spat on her doorstop for luck and overcharged her for bread and meat. What else but a witch's heavy laughter made the udders on the herd overflow and run like piss? The villagers shivered at the noise and put their fingers deep in their children's ears and bottled the milk. It tasted sweeter than honey. Unnatural. They ran Grandmother out of town by slapping her breasts until they bruised and bled. She shielded her tender daughter as best she could, but they caught the little one with short legs, cast her to the ground and marveled at the stones embedded in her face.

Grandmother and mother went to the next village over to try again.

When the daughter was grown and Grandmother dead, Father said her mother flogged herself with a whip of braided horsehair and dull nails. She put her jagged back on display in the square each morning, and the villagers wept at the sight. They made garlands of magnolia and lily of the valley for her hair. They commissioned a stronger whip of leather and glass. Madonna, they called her. Notre Dame. They bowed their heads and asked her blessings. They rolled loaded die to take her to their rooms each night and watch the vicious act with their belts undone. When she put on a child they gripped their hair and wailed and wondered how it could be. When her daughter was born her back convalesced to pink baby skin. The villagers could not look upon her without violent retching, so removed was their desire from her skin, and so she put on a shift of pale tulle and went into the woods alone.

Father said he took her into the swell of his own home because he was a kind man of means and because he did not like his own children, nor his wife's narrowed eyes. He bounced her on his knees and lanced the round blisters on her hands from churning the daily butter. She grew quiet and beautiful and obedient, and he grew to love her.

When she asked, her father said it was the black-eyed devil come round to ask for her hand. Of course, her father did not give his favorite away. He gave his other daughters, the one with horse teeth, the one with the red birthmark, the one with a single eye, and tossed out his wife as well. Then he placed a heavy crucifix around his adopted daughter's neck and on every wall so everywhere she looked there was suffering.

Father wept and said, "it's because you're tainted with your grandmother's curse, your mother's blight. It is on your hands and arms. Everyone who looks at you can see where you've come from. The devil has come to collect his own." She cupped her hands to catch her father's tears, and he used fresh soap and sandpaper to scrub her fingers and elbows raw. She raised the salt water over her head and poured it over her body to burn away the rest.

Father said he shut her away in his bedroom to safeguard her from the villagers, who would see her lineage in her arms. Roused by the devil, they would tear her apart. She was safest under covers. She was safest without candlelight. She was safest against the swell of father's fat belly, big enough to hold her still and keep her warm.

When she asked, he told her not to ask anymore.

When she acted, she took the dull butter knife she hid in her skirts and put it to the place of elbow and bone. Slow she brought it down, slow she carved, low she moaned when it ripped muscles and fractured bone. Then the locked door shook and whined on its metal hinges and burst open. Behind it was the man her father called devil, all long hair and pale eyes. With her permission, he took the sharp axe on his belt and swiftly removed her other arm. He watched her arrange her arms with her toes on the pillows. One vertical. One horizontal. Meeting in the middle. She laughed when he took her in his arms and carried her down the stairs, out of the house, through the village, and into the dark woods.

A Woman
With No Arms

There is a woman in my orchard. My first thought is to load my rifle and shoot her for trespassing, but I notice she has stumps where she should have elbow. Poor thing must have birthed weird, or been hurt before, and there is nothing my gun could do to her that hasn't already been done, except end it, which might be a kindness.

She stares at my lemons for hours, and I understand her obsession. I've won awards all across the county for their plumpness, their shade and their sour bite. No one grows them better than I do because no one knows my secret: my wife and daughter shit into a bowl under the sink, and I save it until there is enough to spread with fish heads and mulch. There's love in the process, and no one has yet been able to replicate it, because they haven't got women who can discharge like I do.

When night falls, and she makes to leave, I go to her and tell her I'll pick a lemon for her if she wants, free of charge, beautiful and bright and yellow. I pluck a fat one and hold it up to her mouth, but she only looks at me like I have offended, bares her teeth and walks away.

That, I think, is the end of armless women.

But she is there the next day, staring at the same tree, her mouth open like a split peach, tongue protruding from her lips. I go out to her and offer her another lemon, but she responds as she did the day before, and leaves.

My daughter, curious and eight, tells me that the woman reminds her of what sorrow must look like, and that should be her name. I tell her that's a rude thing to call a person, and she makes to argue with me, but instead she grabs her belly and runs to the bathroom. Save every bit, I tell her, your output hasn't been great lately.

When the armless woman is there in the morning, I tell her she better leave, after all she is on private property, and she ought to take what is kindly offered and be on her way. If she liked what she tasted she could buy her own in the market, only the first is freely offered. She looks at me like I am some unfathomable, rotten thing.

Then, she smiles.

Smiling stretches her neck, and it continues to lengthen far beyond what a human neck should, the skin moving and expanding but not tearing, lifting her head up towards my lemons. Her neck is as long as what is left of her arms, those odd stumps, and she stops her growing once her lips touch the skin of my lemon, and she bites into it with a little growl and rips it from the branch. She squeezes it between her teeth and sucks. Some lemon-wet dribbles down her chin, but her eyes are all daring. She spits the rind at my feet when she finishes, nothing left but yellow skin and bite.

At the window, my daughter peeks her head out and laughs at how wrong she was. That woman's name was not sorrow, not at all, but she won't tell me what the woman's name is, like it's a private joke she will not share.

An Old Woman
with Silver Hands

I had my hands cut off as a child. That is, of course, half a lie, for one was cut off by another's swift whack of an axe. But I did the first one myself. I would have done the second too, except my teeth were not strong enough then to hold the blade. They're strong enough now, and sharp. They must be, for they serve all my purposes: biting, writing, eating, climbing. I'd walk with them too, but I'm too old to give up my feet.

My teeth have taken on so many other tasks that they have lost their original purpose: to shape the air in my mouth into words. Too long ago, in the night, after years of sharpening themselves on sticks and rocks and lemons, they hungered and bit off my tongue. That I swallowed like everything else, and thought nothing of it at the time: who would I speak to, with no hands? And who would speak to me, a woman who built fire with flint and molars?

Even if I could speak, I would have nothing to say. I am happy to no longer add to the world. Now, I only consume, and I discard. And I walk, so far I walk, on feet that must give out soon.

Before they do, I follow a light in the distance, and I think the light will be the last I see, as that is what I always heard in the stories when I was a girl: a light, brighter than fireflies swarming in your eyes, and then the great nothing. This light is no insect, but a house so lit it seems like it is burning from the inside. As I move closer I can see it is not on fire, as I first believed, but inside are two figures, a woman and her little daughter, and they are melting blocks of silver down in a great furnace. They take hammers to it and bend the silver into all sorts of beautiful things: wrist cuffs and chains for the neck, dainty rings, and even a bowl to collect something as precious as milk.

I thought of leaving them to their art, but the little girl saw me spying in the window and tugged her mother over to the door to open it.

"Grandmother," the woman politely said. "You must be cold. Come inside for a time and warm up. You can pay us in stories of what you have seen and the wisdom you have learned from it."

The daughter was not yet old enough to know her manners, and she gaped at my stumps. I went inside, for I was cold and very tired. I opened my mouth to show them the rotting stump of what was my tongue and closed it when it seemed like the daughter would cry for the pity of it all. Foolish, foolish and kind thing.

"It matters little," the mother said. "We will play you music instead."

I watched them for a time and marveled at their skill, how they could make such beautiful noises, like birds and boulders, from just simple hammers and fine silver.

"Grandmother," the daughter said to me, "let us make you a pair of silver hands. They'll be so beautiful that a prince will cry when he sees them."

I scoffed at that, but little noise came from my throat. What use had I of a prince's tears, so near to the end as I was? With what was left of my arms, I directed the girl to put the silver in the fire and heat it. She did so willingly, but when she pulled it out I grasped it between my stumps and took it to my teeth. I bit and peeled away at the edges until it was the shape I desired. The girl watched in horror as the silver burned down my lips, but I'd cut off my own hand when I was her age, and so little could hurt me now.

As shaped as I could make it, I handed it back to her to put into the fire. She did so with shaking tongs, and when it came out I knelt down in front of her and opened my mouth wide. She knew, darling child, what I wanted, and burned the silver tongue onto the back of my throat.

Her mother crossed herself and called her daughter over, but the girl was too excited to obey.

"Speak now, Grandmother! Tell us who you are and what you have seen!"

I opened my mouth to tell her but found that I must have forgotten what the words should be, and how to make them. All that poured out of my mouth was laughter, a noise that reverberated off the silver and filled the whole house with its pleasure.

They All Could Have Loved You Until You Ate That Child

As a boy, Tarrare always ate more than his weight. His parents thought they were in some sort of messed up fairy tale the old women used to titter on about—the boy who ate his family out of house and home and did not gain a fat pound—and so they did the responsible thing: they kicked his bones and skin out. He cried and said it was cruel of them to do such a thing to their own blood. His mother almost took him back when she saw the water in his eyes, but her husband pointed out the boy was stuffing handfuls of dirt into his mouth, and so they shut and locked the door.

He walked and ate whatever he found—scraps of meat stolen from butchers and crusts of bread left on plates from the mid-day meal—but he was so hungry he ate the leather off his shoes, and then the cloth off his back. A group of wandering thieves and prostitutes found him with the cuff of his pants in his mouth, gnawing, and since they found this funny they asked him to join them. He made his coin putting all sorts of things into his mouth and swallowing: living snails and toads, the handle of a dagger, a virgin's nightgown, tree bark, and, when he had a rich patron who wanted to test his limits, a meal large enough to feed a small army, which he dined on merrily in one sitting and then asked for more. The patron looked under the table to make sure the food was not hidden and it was all a magnificent trick, but there was no trace of it anywhere, except in the air when Tarrare belched.

"Your shit must be a sight to behold," the patron admired, and promptly kicked Tarrare out, as he had started gumming the table.

The patron had ties to the military, and when he met with the General for drinks, he told him about the curious man he met who could eat anything. The General was intrigued and immediately snatched Tarrare up, saying he would feed him whatever he liked and as much as he liked so long as he swallowed a few sealed documents whole. Then, he was to take them across enemy lines and deliver them to his men in the thick of it. The General could have done this himself, but he mused that an expert of digestion would be better suited to this line of work. Tarrare was not sure he wanted this at first, but then the General offered him a bone, and he took the job with a patriotic flair.

Swallowing the letters was the easy part, but he had cramps in enemy territory. Their dirt was unlike the dirt from home, and when he shoved it into his mouth he rolled over in pain and immediately shat himself. That was how the enemy found him, digging through his own waste and trying to shove the letters back down. They laughed and took him to their General, and because Tarrare was a coward who offered state secrets for bread, the General rolled his eyes, aimed his rifle at him and pretended to fire until Tarrare cried.

"Go back home," this General told him. "And don't get involved in matters that don't concern you."

And so Tarrare returned, hungry and failing to live up to the goals of his nation, which he was not quite sure what they were setting out to accomplish, but he felt proud of it all the same. At least the dirt at home didn't make him sick. He returned to his General with his head low.

"It's a shame," said the General, clipping off the ends of his fingernails until they were blunt points. "I knew you were talented, but a man of one talent is not much of a man at all, is he?"

Then Tarrare began to weep, and the General sighed. "Now, now. No reason to be sad about it. Not all of us can be fully formed men— why, that would make for a very sorry world indeed. No conflict, no confusion, no oddities. And you are an oddity. You should embrace that."

The General was overcome by his own magnanimity and thought he might share this later with his wife, and definitely his mistress, so that they too could know what sort of man he was. Then he noticed that Tarrare was popping the nail clippings into his mouth and decided that it was a bit all too much and sent him to hospital.

The nurses were kind to him. They saw a poor hungry thing and gave him their lunches and bathed all the dirt from his body. They turned their heads away when he lapped up the bathwater, and gently scolded him when he tried to chew on the bathtub. They assigned him to Dr. Boyle, who was the expert on all mad things. The doctor took one look at him, took a longer look at his pen as it disappeared down Tarrare's throat, and then an even longer look at Tarrare's feces, which appeared normal.

"Remarkable," he said.

Tarrare shook his head. "I don't want to be like this. I just want to be normal."

"I'll do my best to help you," Dr. Boyle said.

Dr. Boyle decided on an extreme form of treatment: starve the man until his appetite corrected itself. Dr. Boyle locked him in a room and only put water through the door, and no matter how much Tarrare cried and how much he howled, the nurses were under strict orders not to let him out, but every time they passed by the door they had to put their hands to their eyes, lest they create their own water for him. When Dr. Boyle checked on him later, Tarrare was little but skin and bones.

"Now that the madness is starved out, we'll put you on a proper diet."

They fed him three practical meals of fruit and honey, soft boiled eggs, bread and cheese and a vegetable soup, and a little salad with a pastry for dessert. These he ate with all the manners he had garnered from watching others consume, and they all applauded his recovery. Never mind that at night the nurses found him sucking on the wounds of old Mr. Abel, who had sores from an infection on his right leg. They didn't like Mr. Abel much, as he was always putting his hands where they shouldn't be or yelling for better bread. Never mind that once they found Tarrare drinking blood from the collection vials, because it was just a little liquid, and recovery is a process, not instantaneous. Never mind that once they found him chewing on an arm in the morgue—the arm was dead and couldn't feel anymore anyway. As long as there were long sleeves at the funeral, who would mind?

But they had to mind when the baby went missing. Mrs. Lamar was inconsolable after her child disappeared from the nursery. Wasn't it enough that she had suffered to push it out and then to have the hospital lose it? It was all a bit too much. The nurses scrambled and checked every corner that they could but found no trace of the babe, until one of them found a rattle in Tarrare's stool and beat him with it.

"How could you!" she cried. "A baby is an angel and has done nothing to deserve your cruelty, you selfish man."

Tarrare denied ever being cruel but said he was so hungry he didn't even know what he was eating anymore, only that he felt he had a great hole inside of him that he had to keep filling and filling and filling up, and nothing ever seemed to make his want fade. How could anyone know what it was like to never be satisfied, to have people talk of being full, of being in a state when there was nothing more they desired to taste, even for a moment? How could they understand, when inside him he felt only a great emptiness, a gulf that stretched from his core and seemed to swallow all of him, and no thing on earth could plug it, not rocks nor bread nor even the gentle caress of a woman. He was a great mystery to himself, and he had no idea how to solve it.

"Get out," she said, beating him again for good measure. "I hope someone eats you. See how you like it."

And so poor Tarrare found himself all alone on the streets again. He made well enough for a time eating rocks and flowers, but no book he encountered (before he swallowed each page) had any answers for him, and no wise man or woman could tell him what he could eat to sate, and they were furious when he chewed the hems of their robes. He then did the only decent thing he could think of to do. He put up a sign that said, "Free Meal to a Hungry Mouth" and laid down beside it. Eventually, he hoped, someone would come across it and swallow him whole, and then perhaps he would know satisfaction.

For Tarrare, satisfaction did not come. He died there, finally ending his hunger, and soon even his little sign abandoned him, blown away in a particularly strong gust. His body was taken to the hospital for dissection, and Dr. Boyd was particularly pleased, for cutting him open had been his first inclination for curing, though he knew the procedure had a small chance of survival. Now he could do as he pleased, and he chopped Tarrare in two to see what was wrong. At first, he noticed the man's throat was a bit larger than it should be, and his lungs a bit too heavy, though that did not explain much. Yet, where the stomach should be, there was only a great emptiness: not that it was missing, but that it was never there at all. Curious, Dr. Boyd stuck his finger into that emptiness, and it gulped and gargled and swallowed the good doctor whole.

A Tale of
Two Adoptions

"Your father was an elk, but you were born without horns. One night, a man who shared your nose came into your room while your parents, below you, tucked into warm milk and rum. He offered to tie sticks to your head with duct tape and a hot glue gun. "There are bones inside of you," he told you. "How do you know who you are if you cannot see them?"

* * *

A woman lost her daughter in the deep woods. She cried up and down the trunk of every tree until her arms collapsed and she could not lift herself anymore. Kind folks said her daughter was a butterfly now, as all girls are who walk starless roads. Kinder folk brought her the skull of a rabbit. The transformation of girls makes for strange objects, and what was taken away from a mother must be given back.

* * *

When the horns do break the skin at the top of your head your mother wept and died. Your father refused to bury her in the ground with the worms. He placed her body on the bed where you were not conceived and where you were not born. The skin sloughed off her face like runny jelly, followed by the muscle and the fat that once perked her cheekbones. Her skull was as round and smooth as a bright, white ball.

* * *

The daughter was found before she became dust and bones in that dark wood, but not by her mother. A curious doe sniffed at her palm and lead her to the other side of the woods. Not intentionally. It was walking that way and the girl followed. When she emerged into the sunlight a group of flesh-sellers put a blue ribbon around her neck and passed her off as an orphan to a lonely couple, though her mother was still alive, though her mother now dressed the skull of a rabbit in a child's hat and painted its front two teeth pink.

* * *

When your father died on an island—hunting trip, he told you, but you know he went to tie a cord around his neck—you carried his bones back on a boat made of wood and red paint. The fish followed you for some time, but they swam off when you hit rock. You buried what was left of your parents together in their backyard. The house you sold, because it stunk. Where they rest, no grass grew, no flower spread, no ant marched. You could take their story and make it your own, as all stories end up buried in the earth one day, but not yet. Not yet. You still do not know where you come from. You do not know if that matters.

* * *

She cut the ribbon off of her neck on her twelfth birthday, before it threatened to strangle her. The two who purchased her, though they would not approve of it being spoken of in that way, wrapped her in silk threads they'd cultivated in their abdomens. It was warm in those threads, like a cocoon, and above her they crisscrossed threads back and forth so when she looked up at the dark sky, it seemed as if they had hung the stars just for her. "Little rabbit," they told her, "we will love you forever."

* * *

The man returned to you when the bones on your head brushed the ceiling of your little car. "You can't hide them forever," he said to you after you offered him a cup of warm milk and rum. You thought you could. In fact, you had become something of a hat connoisseur. He shook his head and said you looked ridiculous. No one was fooled. "Relax," he told you. So you did, because you did not know what else to do. The moment the muscles in your arms and legs went lax the bones in your head broke through your skull, cracked it in half like it was an eggshell, and from the remains stepped a different you, all fur and snout and bones as sharp as knives. "Is this real?" you asked the man in a voice that was your voice, but not, but was. "You tell me," he said, but you had no answer.

* * *

Years went by before the two of you met. She came to you in a dress of spider silk, and you had taken to wearing ribbons of gold and silver on your antlers. She told you she never found her mother, the one who had lost her long ago, but she remembered her every time she had to file down her two front teeth when they grew too long. "Did you look for her?" you asked, and she only half-smiled. You gave her a cup of milk, though she said she preferred water, but she drank it anyway. "I think," she said after a bit, "we have strange bodies. How long will you spend searching for where they came from?" You did not have an answer for that, because you did not know. She carefully removed the ribbons from your antlers and tied your palms together with them. "What would we make?" you ask her, and she smiles and smiles and shrugs. "Something new," she said, and that was as good an answer as any.

How One Girl Played at Slaughtering

Once, in a city long forgotten, some young boys and girls between the ages of five and six were playing make-believe with one another. After some discussion, they decided to play butcher. One girl was to play the butcher, another the cook; a young boy was to be the cook's assistant, and another young boy was to be the pig. The cook's assistant was to catch the blood of the pig in a tiny bowl, and this blood would be used to make sausages. As they agreed, the butcher-girl fell on the pig-boy with a little knife, and the assistant cook caught the blood in the bowl. The girl started to carve up the pig-boy's body but had trouble because her knife was so small.

As it happened, a Man of Words was walking by and saw the children playing. Appalled, and gagging, he grabbed the butcher-girl and took her into the House of Many Men of Words. There they gathered and wrung their hands over the sorry mess, for they could not decide if it had merely been a game gone too far. Then, one Man of Words took a shiny gold coin from his pocket and a blood-red apple from the kitchen and told them that they would test the girl. They would offer her both, and if she took the apple she was to be deemed a child, and let go. If she took the coin, then she was all grown up, hiding in the body of a petite thing, and they would kill her. One man held them both before her, and she studied them with intent. Then, she laughed and grabbed the apple. She took a bite of it, looking them each in the eye as she did, and licked the juice from her lips. She offered the apple back to them with an open palm, and though some were tempted, none dared reach for it. Because they were Men of Their Words, they had to let her go, and off she went, giggling and making merry as only a child can. But each man in that house fell into an uneasy sleep that night, wondering what would have happened had they taken a bite.

The Skins of Strange Animals

Of the two of them, Todd was more upset when the baby bled out. Beyond the physical pain, which was great, there was no innate strain of motherhood in Cora that inspired regret. When she held the plastic stick with the pink lines up to Todd's face, she knew she did not particularly desire the change, but she supposed she would shoulder the child as one burdens all the milestones: the first menses, marriage, tax audits, and picking out the gravestone your mother might have wanted. Once, she had read that the brain released chemicals after a child is born so mothers, tired from the endless wailing, would be brainwashed into loving the fragile things and not smother them for one night of uninterrupted sleep. Evolution's protective flip switch: it's not screaming, it's my little baby-love.

Cora was ten weeks along, give or take, when she began spotting red. Todd drove her to the hospital, murmuring about reading an article online that clinically explained it was not necessarily serious, this happens, but he knuckled the wheel and glanced at her belly at stop signs. The doctor ran a cold machine over her and looked at Cora's neck when she said there was no heartbeat.

Did she want it taken out, or did she want it to slide out naturally? It might take several weeks on its own.

Todd gripped her hand while the doctor explained that it was a missed abortion, and the tissue—tissue, now—would have to slide out one way or another. It could not remain.

Around eleven that night her belly constricted and released. Cora sat on the toilet to piss, she thought she had to piss, and felt the pain wind up her abdomen. When she relaxed her muscles, she felt the splash. There was so much blood, and a small sac.

Todd hovered in the doorway. "I'll take care of it," he said. "You don't have to look."

She'd already looked.

She waited in the hallway for the toilet to flush, holding a clump of toilet paper between her legs, fearing she would stain the carpet, not knowing how long it would take to fully empty out. She heard the faucet running and peeked in. Todd was gently, lovingly, washing off the sac. He must have plucked it out of the water. It was clear and gelatinous with a dark center.

It was an intimate moment she was not supposed to see, Todd holding that part of her, of him, that should have been kept inside. Cora supposed she ought to cry but felt drained enough just from crying out between her legs, and that was enough wetness for one body.

She never knew what he did with it. She never asked.

Later, he bent down on one knee and gave her a golden band wrapped in diamonds.

"Why now?" she asked.

"It's not the child," he said.

That was the first secret moment with him, the one that made Cora think she might love him.

* * *

He only told this story to Cora once, but she remembered it and carefully cultivated it, like it was her own memory. When he was nine, Todd had fallen in mad love at a petting zoo. His parents had dragged him in an effort to show him that he was capable of making connections, even if it was just for a moment, even if it was with a dumb animal, bred to be gentle and accommodating. Todd found making friends with other children difficult, though he had trouble making enemies as well. The other children didn't bully him or shove him into a locker or call him names. They acted as if he was not there at all and, if they were partnered with him for a craft project or asked to work together on spelling or addition in groups, they stared at him like they had never seen him before.

Todd liked the ducklings, their strange flat feet, and the way they would run from him but look behind to see if he was still chasing them. The quarters for the feed machine jangled in his pocket. A goat chewed on his shirt and he let it, too afraid to move, too afraid that it would walk away to any of the other children who made little piles of food around them and waited for the animals to clamor up.

There was another girl there with braided brown hair, shaking as she brought her hand up to pet the backside of a graying donkey. The animal was fat and old. The hair around its eyes and mouth were white. Some of its teeth were black and chipped, but it wiggled its shagged tail back and forth.

Todd must have made a noise, because the girl looked at him, really looked at him. She had dark eyes and a smudge of dirt on her cheek, gaps between her teeth. Todd shambled over to her. He didn't know what to say to her, afraid that anything he did would wake her up and she would remember that he was invisible and forget how to see him.

The other children were so odd to him, the way they moved and spoke without any sort of consideration for the angle of their bodies.

During crafts, they snaked their hands into the crayon bins and were happy with whatever they grabbed. The lions in their coloring books were pink or green, whatever was the closest color at hand. They chose so easily. He tried to mimic them, closing his eyes and reaching into the bin and pressing whatever was in his hand onto the paper.

"That's very nice, Todd," his teacher murmured when she walked by. "But try coloring in the lines?"

Don't think, he told himself, just act for this girl who could see him. Todd reached out and grabbed one of her braids—soft and wild, loose strands tickled his palm. She screamed, the wild yelp of a surprised and indignant child, and flailed her hands, hitting the donkey on its backside. It bellowed, a hoarse choking sound, and kicked its leg out, knocking Todd to the ground.

He briefly remembered hearing the brown-haired girl crying, then the long shadows of his parents falling over him, putting their hands on his face.

"Breathe, honey," his mother's voice kept repeating. "Come on, just breathe, breathe for me, baby."

He tried, he really did. Thought back to the times he'd puffed out his chest and held the air in when the kids in class ignored him and he thought if he just made himself a little bit larger, took up a bit more room, they would see him. Each time he tried it burned, each time he tried to move his chest ached.

They kept him in the hospital for a week, his parents alternatively holding his hand, talking to doctors who said things like cracked ribs and collapsed lung, and screaming over the phone at the owners of the petting zoo about lawyers and emotional damage.

He'd have that half-round scar on his chest for his whole life.

He asked what happened to the little girl with the short dark hair, but his parents couldn't really say.

Later, he overheard his parents whispering that the beast had been put down.

After he had finished his story, his hand resting on her thigh, she knew that this was the moment she could love him. Love, after all, was having secrets you only told one other person. Of course, she told her friends this story. But only so that they could know the fullness of his character and approve.

* * *

It was Marjorie who inadvertently convinced Cora to accept the proposal, a week after he had given her the ring and she told Todd she would consider it, "Let me think on it", but wore the band on her finger. She asked Winter and Summer their opinion. They were children of overgrown hippies who met online in a support group for parents gone to seed, and stayed together because they both voted Republican for fiscal reasons but hated pearls.

"Well, of course you should," Winter told her, holding Summer's hand in his own. "He's so good with kids."

"Can't knock a guy who is good with kids," Summer repeated.

"Spends his weekends coaching field hockey?" Winter asked.

"Softball," Cora said.

"Yeah. And doesn't he co-lead that Girl Scout troop? You couldn't pay me to pretend to enjoy gluing sticks together while someone's crying because little Martha is being a bitch. Again."

"Is that what they do," Summer said, intently staring at Cora. "Glue shit for hours?"

"Sometimes."

"Christ," said Summer. "What a saint."

Cora remained unconvinced at this praise of Todd's character. Summer and Winter had been aching for her to marry any of the men she had slept with for longer than a week. They were fond of throwing parties and claimed her single status made the married guests twitch away from her, like she was radioactive and bright.

Later, Cora went to Marjorie's and sat in the old woman's kitchenette. They talked together near the open window so Marjorie could smoke. The neighbor, a plump woman who went running every day but slogged back after an hour with a sack of fast food, fake-coughed whenever Marjorie was on the landing, lighting a cigarette with the dying ember of another. Marjorie was an odd choice for Cora's godmother, particularly because she was an atheist, but she was Cora's mother's dearest friend and the only one who had never married. There was a part of Cora that suspected her mother really believed that all woman just wanted something to nurture, even if it didn't come out of their own bodies.

"I thought I was crazy," Marjorie said, "watching a documentary about penguins. You know there's all those kids who don't have enough to eat and here we are in Antarctica training our cameras on little waddlers, as if we're somehow going to find some mystery about the human experience from birds. They can't even fly."

Marjorie was flinging herself around the kitchen in the way that only a woman who had no real idea what the space was for could do. She opened cabinets and closed them, opened the fridge door, moved condiments around, checked their dates, frowned, and put them back. She settled for boiling water on the stove, one of her few skills, and sat a tray of assorted teas—most likely swiped from one hotel's continental breakfast or another—in front of Cora.

"It's a six-part series. On penguins. Can you imagine?" Marjorie gestured at the diamond on Cora's finger. "That's a pretty thing," she said. She did not sound excited.

"He'll never leave me," said Cora. "That's a point in his favor, right?"

Marjorie cough-laughed. "There's trouble right there. Thinking you can make a thing permanent just by wishing it."

Yet Marjorie couldn't understand that it had been six months before Todd had let Cora see the scar on his chest. They'd rolled together in the bed in complete darkness, and he undressed and redressed before she could see what was there. He held her hands above her head and laid heavy on her forearms when she tried to feel his skin or turned her around and took her from behind. When she demanded he show her himself, all of him, he had stilled on the bed. Eyes up at the ceiling. Arms limp at his side. She dragged the shirt over his head like he was a child, pausing at the horseshoe scar. She touched it with her fingers and he shuddered. He looked so ashamed, and so grateful, when she ran her tongue over the smoothness that had stretched as his body expanded.

"Men with scars are the kind you fuck, but they don't stay put."

"You're being ridiculous," Cora said, steeping her teabag and watching the water darken. Marjorie did not believe in spending time on beverages. A quick heat up and a quick swallow.

"They don't. They've survived being opened up. So they'll keep doing it, over and over. It's a psychosis. It might not be another woman, or another man, but it will be something. Maybe he'll spend hours taking pictures of his cock and slipping it into letters online. Or he'll skydive, try to make new scars."

That was what Marjorie could never understand about Todd: his grateful looks that she saw him and responded.

"Anyway," said Marjorie, "a grown man afraid of donkeys? Don't you find that a bit peculiar?"

Cora accepted his proposal that night.

* * *

It wasn't that Cora was terribly afraid of being abandoned, or cheated on, by Todd. If he did, he did, and that was the way of people in long-term relationships. Their bodies wavered as their eyes wandered; the monotony of laundry and dishes and appointments dragged. Yet she couldn't imagine him working up the courage to take off his shirt with anyone else, and so even if he fucked someone else, she was sure that only she would have had that intimate part of him on her lips.

It made her feel special, that only she knew that part of him.

* * *

Cora was pregnant again shortly after they married. She'd been careful with her birth control, same time every day, even though it was eight at night and sometimes she downed it with a cold beer. Then she forgot to be careful, and when the lines showed up on the plastic strip Todd called and made an appointment.

"I hope it's a boy," he told her. Cora was hurt by this, and not entirely sure why.

There were a range of exams to go through to make sure the child stayed in her as long as possible. Hormonal imbalances, genetic disorders, physicals. She was asked if she smoked or drank much. Neither, of course, not when she was carrying someone else, but Todd stared at her and mouthed, "Marjorie," but Cora knew that Marjorie would risk the ire of her neighbor for her and smoke outside.

Cora made sure that Todd got tested too and sat nervously in the room as the doctor questioned him about his medical history. Was there anything wrong with his family's blood or their chromosomes, those letters arranged in what looked to her like a random order, but must have meant something to those who knew how to read it? Were the kidneys alright, did his grandparents have diabetes? Did all their hearts beat like metronomes, or did they skip every once in a while?

She imagined they must have been looking at that four letter code to find something that says how far the scars go, and what sort of scars were light enough to form something like a healthy child.

But what if whatever is wrong is written so intrinsically on the smallest part, that it cannot be seen, and we need a stranger to hold us up to the microscope and tell us what our true selves really look like?

All normal, of course. Both of them.

* * *

Cora could not say if the pregnancy was easier or harder than an average one. She scanned the books and the internet confessionals and mommy blogs and found the information overwhelming and competitive. Todd was ever attentive, and Winter and Summer cooed at him and said how very much they were jealous, which Cora supposed she may have appreciated once, but now felt too tired to feel much of anything at all.

After they found out it would be a girl, even though Todd asked the doctor to be sure and wave the ultrasound all around Cora's belly to find some sort of elusive penis that was not going to sprout between its legs, she put her hand on his and he settled.

"You'll love her anyway, won't you?" she asked, annoyed at herself for being worried.

"Of course," Todd said, squeezing her hand back. "That's not what I'm afraid of. You know, it's just…a man wants to see himself in a boy."

* * *

Fiona was a beautiful child, carried to term, all six pounds and seven ounces of her. She came out with Todd's face, except scrunched and bloody, and without any scars, except the one that all people would eventually share on their navel, when the last bit of Cora would wither and blacken and fall off. They put her in Cora's arms and she was so depleted she didn't love her daughter at first. Love seemed too much energy then. She wanted to sleep. Marjorie, who stumbled in between her many smoke breaks, nagged a nurse until they took the child to the nursery over Todd's protests.

"Let mom have her rest," Marjorie said in a voice which brooked no argument. She then slipped a wrapped package into Cora's bed. It was soft, and Cora fell asleep on it.

Later, when Todd was looking over his child, tentatively touching her balled up fist, Cora knew that she did love her daughter.

Cora forgot about Marjorie's gift until they were at home. She went in first while Todd struggled with his unfamiliarity with car seats, leaving her to drag their hospital bag in the door and dropping it. She pulled out the gift and squeezed it between her hands.

Todd came in with Fiona a moment later. "What's that?" he asked.

"It's from Marjorie. I forgot to open it at the hospital." Cora peeled away the tape as carefully as she could, being raised in a family that reused wrapping paper. She immediately regretted not doing so privately. It was a stuffed donkey.

"Is this her idea of a joke?" Todd asked, stiff and hard-lipped. Betrayed.

"You know how she is," Cora said. "She doesn't have family, so she has to poke the replacement."

"Throw it out."

"I can't do that."

"I don't want that in the house."

"It's just a toy. We'll put it in the nursery closet and trot it out when she's over to make her happy. Okay?"

"That's not funny."

"What?" Cora asked, honestly confused.

"Trot." Todd said, as one would a curse word.

"Oh, come on. It was a slip of the tongue."

When he was out of the room, Cora allowed herself to quietly laugh at the joke.

* * *

Cora did not expect him to be the perfect parent—it was, after all, hard for her to even love a ball of flesh that did little more than shit and cry and break the skin on her breasts—but she did think that he would be better at it than he was. He did not break any of his previous commitments to the daughters of other men, continuing to help out with the Girl Scouts and coaching softball. It was hard for her, the first few years, to not resent his face, wet with sweat and smiling, when he came home dragging the metal bat behind him, exhilarated and clammy. But then he would take her in his arms and kiss her, and Cora loved the smallness of the gesture. Winter and Summer were inclined towards grand ones, hundred rose bouquets that slowly rotted in their bedroom, or spontaneous trips to Europe, or hiring a quartet to sing songs to one another of a love long since dead, but renewed with each verse. No, Cora believed it was better to be happy with smaller things, like the way her daughter laughed when she was in the bath, or the way Todd would fall asleep on the recliner as he watched baseball, a bit of drool at the side of his lips, and smile at her when she woke him and told him it was time for bed.

* * *

She quit her job when Fiona was three years old. Only Marjorie had anything negative to say about it. Summer and Winter believed it was necessary for a mother to be with her child, which made Cora wonder if they had been judging her for not having quit sooner. Todd was equally supportive, though she suspected it was because he did little in terms of childcare and this took the burden off of him. He refused to give up coaching softball or assisting with his local scout troop, which Cora took issue with as it often left her home alone with her toddler, but no matter what argument she posed, Todd would not relent.

"What are you going to do with all that time?" Marjorie asked.

There were arguments to be made, but Cora did not voice them. Raising a child took up her entire day. Doctor's appointments, feeding, cleaning, amusement, sneaking into the shower during naptime, fighting to enroll her in the best preschool they could afford and settling for the second best one, because the first best had a waiting list Cora had not been able to crack. Still, preschool was coming within a year, and that would open up her mornings.

"I'm teaching myself how to sew."

"The domestic arts," Marjorie said, her voice dry.

Cora shrugged. "Todd said I could darn his socks. But I want to make outfits for Fiona. Costumes. Halloween will be fun this year. I was thinking we could be themed. She can be Cinderella and I'll be the fairy godmother."

"And Todd as Prince Charming? If you say so," Marjorie told her. "No man is a prince. Not even the royals."

Fiona played on the floor between them with the stuffed donkey. She loved the damn thing, but because Todd felt so uneasy around it Cora only let her play with it at Marjorie's. It made her dread visiting, because it meant when they left she'd have to take it away from Fiona and stick the stuffed beast in the trunk, which only resulted in sobs and wails the whole drive home, but she was not about to give up her chance to speak to a grown woman during the day.

"I don't know why a man would be afraid of a toy," Marjorie went on. Cora stayed silent, not willing to have this argument again. Marjorie didn't understand the sort of sacrifices that went into a marriage, how most of it was choosing which arguments to have, and which to stay silent on, and which ones required you to sink into yourself until you barely recognized where you went, or what you wanted, and only comfortable dullness remained.

"You're like that penguin," Marjorie said, taking a long drag at the window.

"What penguin?" Cora asked. "Are you watching documentaries again?"

"You learn a lot from animals. There's this one. In Antarctica. It started walking to the middle of the continent. There's nothing there, you know. Just ice and mountains. Damn thing was going to die. The people filming it aren't supposed to get involved, but they did with this one. They turned him around, towards the ocean, thinking he was just confused about which way had the food. But the damn thing just switched direction and walked off towards the center again. Walked off to die all alone out there."

"And this penguin is me?" Cora asked.

"Stubborn," Marjorie noted.

Cora watched Fiona trot the donkey across the floor, cooing. "You need to expand your viewing habits. But maybe that can be the backup idea. I'll make penguin costumes for all of us."

* * *

Fiona was five when Cora began to suspect. "I think Todd is having an affair," she told Winter and Summer over drinks on a rare night out when she had convinced Todd on one of his non-coaching nights to babysit.

Summer and Winter exchanged looks. "Darling, are you sure?" Winter asked as Summer grasped her hands with an alacrity that made Cora wonder if they had been waiting for this moment and practiced a routine.

Summer hummed. "It's not the end of everything if he is, of course. We believe you if you say so. Plenty of marriages survive a little in flagrante delicto."

Winter nodded. "It's true. Remember Ruben and Rachel? She was tipping every dark-haired man who came across her line of vision, but Ruben never left her. I think they were happier for it."

"Oh yes, that's true," Summer agreed. "Though I always assumed Ruben was gay and that took the pressure off. But we shouldn't be jumping to conclusions. Do you have any proof?"

Cora shook her head. "No, not really. Not like, in the traditional sense. He doesn't seem to be bonding with Fiona. He rarely spends any time with her and when he does he says he can't because of that damn donkey Marjorie bought her. So I hide it whenever he's home. Which is damned difficult because Fiona just screams and screams for it. I have to slip it into her bed when he's not looking. She loves the thing."

"Oh, that's not uncommon. You're just going a bit mad because you're home all the time. Stir crazy-baby."

"She's five."

"That's still a baby."

Winter patted her hand. "You need to put your foot down and tell him that you want him to spend more time with Fiona. And you. You can't just let him go out and have a life without you: you're the mother of his daughter."

"He seems like he's scared of her whenever he's with her. He looks terrified."

"Men." Winter and Summer nodded, with Winter seeming to take no offense. "They're not good with kids."

"I don't think that's true," Cora said. "He's good with the softball girls. They love him. They write him cards. Hell, he received Valentine's cards from a few of them last year. They're on the fridge."

"Ah, crushes," Summer said, leaning her head on Winter's shoulder. "Do you remember those?"

"No," Winter said, laughing.

* * *

In September, the girls won their softball championship game. It also marked a year since Todd and Cora had been intimate. Todd insisted they celebrate at their own house with the girls, and so Cora planned to make a spread of healthy snacks: cucumber slices with dill sauce, homemade hummus and pita, glazed carrots and rolled up ham with cheese, but Fiona had been sleeping worse than usual and her teachers said she had been acting out at school—raising her fist to the boys—and so Cora ordered pizza and picked up a few buckets of cheap ice cream at the store.

The girls danced and sang off-key karaoke along with the radio, scarfed pizza or played with Fiona. Todd sat in his armchair while two of the girls sat on either side of him, high-fiving him or begging him to speak to the high school coach about their skills for when they tried out next year. One of them, a brunette with freckles and blue eyes (they all looked fairly similar to Cora, and she struggled to remember their names) put her head on his shoulder and laughed when he said something which she must have found funny.

"Your daughter is so cute," a blonde told her, and Cora smiled at the compliment. "Coach Tee said you make costumes for her?"

"Yeah," Cora said. "She likes to dress up like animals. I've made a butterfly, a duck, and a penguin."

"Oh wow!" said a different blonde, sidling up to them. "Can we see?"

"Oh, sure," said Cora, bored out of her mind and more than willing to show off her handiwork, which she had, she believed, gotten quite good at. "Let me see if I can get her to wear one. Fiona," she called. "Do you want to show everyone your duckie costume?"

Fiona ran over to Cora and nodded her head, which made the two girls clap their hands. Cora reached down and picked her up and began to carry her up the stairs.

"Coach Tee," she heard one of the girls say on her way up. "The downstairs bathroom is occupied and I gotta go. Do you have another one?"

"Let me show you," Todd said, followed by the sound of his body rising from the recliner. "It's upstairs."

Cora went into Fiona's room and closed the door. Fiona asked for her donkey to hold, and Cora, after making her promise that they would leave it in the closet when they went back downstairs, grabbed it from the top shelf and handed it over. Fiona was often irritable when being undressed, and she figured giving in to the request might make it easier.

She managed to take off her shirt with little trouble, though Fiona fidgeted and argued when Cora went to take off her pants.

"You're going to be too hot if you wear this and your duckie costume," Cora told her, even though she had long since figured out that arguing with a child often got her nowhere.

It was a struggle, but Cora managed to get her pants off. There was a new bruise on her thigh, which when they first started to appear had sent Cora into an alarmed meeting with Fiona's teachers, asking them what kind of rough housing they were doing at that school, as well as her doctors to be sure that nothing was medically wrong with the girl, but everyone, including Winter and Summer when she mentioned it, reminded her that kids fall, were rough with one another, and bruised all the time. She eventually let it go once she saw Fiona run around the house in a sugar-craze and bumped her forehead into a door. That bruise had been awkward to explain.

"You need to be more careful," she reminded Fiona, who was hugging the donkey to her chest. "Do you want mommy to kiss it and make it better?"

"No," Fiona said, rubbing her face against the toy.

"Okay," Cora said, holding up the duckie costume. "One foot in at a time."

When Fiona was fully costumed, she made a beeline for the door with the donkey in hand. Cora snatched it right before Fiona managed to make it out the door, and only kept Fiona from protesting by reminding her that she had guests who wanted to see her in all her duckie glory. Fiona ran out, and Cora put the donkey back on the top shelf of the closet, behind a pile of folded clothes. She heard the squeals of delight coming from downstairs. The duckie had been a triumph.

She stopped in the hallway when she saw Todd and the brunette.

He was leaning over her and whispering, and Cora couldn't make out what he was saying. When the girl saw her, her eyes went wide and she ran down the stairs, taking two at a time. Todd turned to look at her.

"What was that?" Cora asked, not sure if she was breathing anymore.

"Didn't want her to get lost," Todd said. "Kids, you know? They go through stuff if you're not careful."

"Yes," Cora said, and watched him retreat back down to the girls.

How old were they, she wondered. Twelve? Eleven?

* * *

That night, after the girls were gone and everything cleaned, she did not say anything more to Todd about it. She did not know what to say, or what to think. It was nothing, certainly, though she stood longer in front of the fridge than normal, looking at the Valentines from the girls and wondering just how deeply they pressed their markers onto the paper to make those red hearts.

She went into Fiona's room to tuck her into bed, making sure to give her the donkey.

"Everyone loved your duckie, darling," she said.

Fiona smiled and cuddled the donkey to her chest.

"Donkey is getting a bit old," Cora said. "Maybe we should get you a new one?"

"No mommy," Fiona said. "Donkey keeps the dreams away."

"What dreams?"

"I don't know."

Cora cajoled, but nothing would budge Fiona to say more.

That night, she had a hard time falling asleep. She wondered if that brunette had seen the scar on his chest, and what a young girl would think of it. A grown man, afraid of a dumb beast.

* * *

"What are you doing for Halloween this year?" Todd asked her, early in October.

"I'm not sure yet," she said. "Maybe pigs? We can go as the three little pigs."

"I'm not wearing a onesie," Todd said to her.

"Maybe just pig ears for you then," she said.

They had not spoken of the girl in the hallway, but Cora was desperate to say something. To have everything she suspected burst out of her, and to hear him laugh with incredulity, so that she could feel foolish and forget.

She remembered the fetus he had pulled from the toilet and held, like it was a precious thing. Before, she had always considered the act something special, one of those grand gestures she was not fond of, but because he had done it privately, it became one of the grandest. How he had lovingly touched it, this thing that was all potential of the two of them, how he must have mourned the loss in such a disgusting and kind way. Much like his scar which he said he showed to no one, save her and his doctor, it was something for them alone. A cornerstone of their marriage. A private thing.

"Mommy," Fiona said, wandering into the living room. "Donkey's ear is broke."

Todd was on his feet faster than she was. "For God's sake, Cora, why does she still have that fucking thing?"

"Mommy," Fiona said, backing away from her father.

"It's just a toy," Cora said.

Todd threw his hands up. "Throw it out."

"No!" Fiona screamed, clutching the donkey, one of its floppy ears loose and held together by thread. "No!"

Todd started towards Fiona, and Cora was on her feet immediately, prepared to do what she did not know she would do. Throw herself at him? Strike him if he went to strike their daughter? Fish the donkey out of the trash if he threw it out? But she was not quick enough, and Todd snatched at Fiona and ripped the donkey from the girl's arms. Its ear, which had been hanging on by threads, tore off entirely. Fiona screamed and screamed, and when she made to go and take it back from him, he pushed her over and she landed with a hard thud, which only made her scream louder.

Cora held Fiona and shushed her, watching as Todd took the donkey outside. When he came back in without it, he looked at the two of them huddled on the floor, shook his head with disgust, and went upstairs.

* * *

Cora slept in Fiona's bed that night. The girl was inconsolable for most of the evening, and Todd had not left their bedroom. Though she had searched the garbage can, she had not found the toy, and she wondered if that was how Todd felt when he pulled that part of her from the toilet: trying to search for something precious in the waste.

"Don't cry," Cora told Fiona. "I'll keep the bad dreams away."

* * *

Marjorie was livid when she was told of what happened to the donkey, but livid for Marjorie was rolling her eyes and smoking two cigarettes in a row.

"I never liked him," she said.

"Marge," Cora said. Stopped, then started again. "Have you ever been happy not knowing something?"

"What do you mean?" Marjorie asked, lighting up her third.

"Like, you suspect something. You suspect something awful, which might be the most awful thing in the world, and if it was true your whole world would be…different. Worse. Like everything would fall apart and every bet you placed would lose."

Marjorie looked at her with such sadness, Cora thought she might break down.

"You remember those penguins?"

"God dammit," Cora said, putting her head in her hands. "I'm so sick of hearing about those penguins."

"Yes well, one more time, and then I won't ever mention them again. Fair?" She took a long drag. "That penguin who went to the center of Antarctica, the one who would not turn around even though there was nothing for him in the center of it except death…that was the easier choice for him. To go into certainty. It would have been harder for him to turn around and go back to the ocean, where any number of things could have snatched his body and ripped him to shreds. Or perhaps he would have starved. Or gotten lost. Or any number of terrible things. Can you imagine what it would be like to have your little body torn apart by a seal? So he took the path where he was blind to everything but his own certain destruction."

Cora closed her eyes. "So you can't win."

"Probably not," Marjorie said with a chuckle. "But you shouldn't go on the path where you know the ending. Where there is no potential for anything else."

* * *

They were talking again, but politely, in a strained way that two people who love one another do when they were still angry but were grounded in history. Small talk, mostly, about their days, how they were feeling after a sip of coffee, if they had a dream the night before (neither of them shared if they did). Fiona was discussed in only the most vague terms: how she was doing in school, if she was eating her vegetables. Cora would have to work a little harder reading with her, as Fiona was struggling to pronounce certain words. Todd made a vague promise about taking them to a kid's movie that weekend, which neither of them cared to see.

Cora knew she should not bring it up, because it wasn't really the thing that ached at her, but she was inclined towards dealing with the past hurts rather than the present ones.

"Remember when Fiona was small, in my belly?" she asked him.

He smiled at her, a genuine smile, one she had not seen for a while, and she realized then the power she held in this moment. She could smile back at him, and they could work at peace, or work on another child, maybe at that moment, scrambling like teenagers to their bed to do it comfortably or even bend down on the floor of the kitchen and pretend at an exuberance their knees had long since stopped accommodating.

"You said you wished she was a boy," Cora said, with a quiet viciousness.

Todd stared at her.

"Why did you say that?" she asked.

"No reason," he said, turning back to his coffee. "It was a dumb thing to say."

Later, when she was curled up with Fiona and reading alongside her, a book about dogs with simple sentences, patiently helping her to pronounce words with three or more syllables, she would be reminded that words, and how you say them, have a kind of power. When Fiona sniffled a little for her donkey, she was reminded that actions do too.

That night, she worked on their costumes.

* * *

Cora invited Summer and Winter, along with Todd's parents and his co-workers, their neighbors, and Marjorie over for a Halloween party. Fiona was upstairs in her room, having promised that she would be quiet and only come out if it was an emergency. Cora had spent the whole week getting ready, putting up decorations, ordering food, and picking up the expensive wine that cost over ten dollars a bottle from the store. She worked every night to finish sewing, measuring, and putting the final furry touches on their costumes. She had not returned to her bed with Todd in this time, but they had been making headway into being more pleasant with one another. She made him coffee in the morning before he went to work and brought it to him in bed. He gave her a chaste kiss on her cheek when he returned home.

"You can't smoke inside," Todd was telling Marjorie, who looked like she wanted to tell him where he could smoke it, but she only nodded her head, which made her witch's hat fall to the floor.

Summer and Winter, never ones to under-dress for any event, came as Harlequin clowns with Venetian masks, which they had picked up after a spontaneous weekend to New Orleans. They were delighting Todd's parents, who had come dressed as pirates complete with stuffed birds on their shoulders and eye-patches, with a waltz. The neighbors and co-workers were a mix of nurses, skeletons, one notable couple who came as a priest and a sexy nun, and Todd who, having not been given a costume by Cora this year, had pasted a sign that said "Pedestrian" to his shirt, which everyone gave him grief over for being so lazy.

Todd pressed his lips to Cora's cheek when she approached, eyeing his parents as he did. "This is a wonderful party," he told her. "Thanks for putting it together."

"I've always loved Halloween," she told him. She took his glass from his hand and took a sip. When she handed it back, there was a smudge of pink from her lips on the rim.

"I'm surprised you didn't dress up this year," he said, then spoke quietly. "I know things haven't been the best between us, lately. And I'm sorry about that. It's childish of me, and I know it, but I can't explain how it feels to remember that…" he put his hand over his chest, where the scar was.

"It's alright," she told him, and meant it. "I understand."

He smiled at her, then, true and gorgeous as he could, that secret smile that was only for her when she made him happy. For a moment, she almost decided not to go through with it, to stay in her dress and keep looking at the center of the continent that was the love she had for him, and move forward without looking behind her, to an ending that she could keep her head down to and push ever onward.

But there were scars on her body, too, the kind where her skin stretched her breasts to store milk for her daughter. Todd was not the only one who bore such things.

"I did make a costume," she said. "I didn't want to wear it when I was putting out the food. I'll go get changed."

"Of course," he said, then turned to the room. "Everyone, Cora is going to show you her latest creation."

Everyone clapped, and she distinctly heard Winter or Summer say, "Finally!"

* * *

It was both not her best work, having been done in something of a hurry, and her favorite. She had learned, from the year of the bee when Todd was working late and she had to go out with Fiona trick-or-treating alone, that when you did full body costumes and had no one to zip you up, you had to put a zipper on the side, not the back. Fiona giggled as Cora zipped her into her miniature version.

"Do you like it?" she asked her daughter.

"Love it!" Fiona said, reaching out to touch her ears, which flopped down on her face.

"Careful with those," Cora said. "They're delicate."

Gathering her daughter into her arms, she walked downstairs into the party. The room, boisterous before she got down there, was quiet now. Todd's parents were exchanging glances with one another, and

Summer and Winter looked at her with confusion, trying to mime their faces into politeness, but clearly struggling with the effort.

Todd's arms hung loosely at his sides, and the wine he was holding slipped through his fingers and fell to the floor. It splattered, like a blood stain, on the carpet. She saw the whites of his eyes and in the quiet of the room, heard the breath he took into his lungs.

Marjorie jumped up from her seat, cackling like the witch she was dressed as, an unlit cigarette dangling from his lips. "Cora, it's simply marvelous. Now what sort of animal would you two ladies be?"

Cora held her grinning daughter higher. "Fiona, tell our guests what we are."

"Donkeys!" her daughter cried, her floppy ear, hanging on by only a few threads, falling on her face.

"That's right," Cora said, looking at Todd. "And what sound do donkeys make?"

"Hee-hah!"

Todd started to back away, to retreat into a corner, but he could only retreat so far before he backed into a wall. Cora moved forward towards him, her daughter in her hands, until his whole body was smashed flat.

"Hee-hah!" Cora shouted along with her daughter, raising her voice high and joyously. "Hee-hah, hee-hah, hee-hah!"

Get Bent

How does a girl dance when her legs are bent at the knee? This is a riddle my grandmother once asked. At the time, I had no answer. My legs were as still as the two beams of the cross, and I dared not do anything but stand as straight as corn.

"You'll have to bend sooner or later," she told me. "All girls get on their knees."

She crushed rose petals in her palm until the red dripped down her arm like a wound. She did this for many weeks, each morning and evening, until her skin was a gnarl of stains. She collected the droplets into a silver bowl. When the liquid neared the brim, she bade me bring her my white shoes and dipped the leather in.

"When you're up there with your head bowed with the rest of them," she told me, a wink creasing her eye, "they'll only be looking at you."

Red shoes needs black stockings and black stockings need a white dress to cover them, but I had no white dress except the one I was to wear on my knees, and so I put it on. I twirled and plied and pirouetted as well as I could, though I had never been trained to do more than lower my eyes. None of us girls were trained beyond the smallest of movements. An eyelash flutter there. A curl of the finger here. Anything more and you'd have green eyes on you.

Green eyes on red shoes was another sort of riddle, but there was a simple answer to that.

The other girls were already on their knees when I arrived at our little church, so the only eyes on me were the priest with the buttoned-up cassock. When he woke up that morning his eyes were blue, like bird eggs, but when they changed the other girls saw—such magic, after all, is only possible through our Lord—they began to weep, for nothing they wore inspired a miracle.

But a miracle is not a miracle unless it spreads as dandelions do in the wind. I bent my legs where bone meets bone and leaped into the air, so high that the girls could see my body over the pews, and more so, they could see my shoes, as bright as rubies, tipped to a point at the toe.

I knew better, but how could I stop, now that I knew all the ways my body could move?

Later, one night after dancing well into starlight, I awoke to my grandmother weeping in the other room, and the hands of my sister-cousins holding me down. The moon was only half full through my window, but it was enough light to see the edges of green in their eyes, and the glint of silver on the dull blades they grasped.

How does a girl dance with only shoes? They asked this to one another that evening. One by one they put my red shoes on over their stockings, but they had never considered bending their knees for anything other than kneeling, and no matter which way they swayed back and forth, they could not dance.

If their hands were not covering my mouth, I could have told them: shoes were not enough, not for twisting, not for crouching, not for leaping. They realized this on their own soon enough, but they did not solve the riddle of how to bend.

They took my legs as well.

Grandmother wept but she did not weep long, not even when, over the small fence around our house, we saw my legs propped in the air, my red shoes bright in the sun, swaying back and forth in a macabre parade. Even with these parts of me, those girls did not know how to dance.

Later, my grandmother would tell me she did not mean me any pain. Later, she would say that a girl with legs as long as I should have been born in a place where girls were not discouraged from knowing what their bodies were capable of. Later, she stood far enough away from me so I could not touch her, and her grimace pulled at her chapped lips until they bled.

Then she brought me another pair of bright red shoes.

"How does a girl get out of bed?" she asked me. "Will you bend again?"

I moved what I could at first. A twist of my neck. The curl of my thumb. Blinked both eyes. My belly could curve inward.

My hands slid into the shoes as easily as my feet. An elbow is not so different from a knee, and mine curved into a fine edge. I could swish. I could reach. I could lift myself into the air.

How does a girl dance with red shoes and no legs? The answer is me.

Mama Had a Baby and Her Head Popped Off

Poor Dada had no glue to put her back together again.

He long suspected Mama was, in the kindest way to describe her, a skin bag to hold the lungs and liver inside. The rest of her was a mystery. Her head flying across the room while he was digging into his egg and pepper breakfast only furthered his belief. She was some thing that transported guts and goo from the market to the kitchen and back again, like a dancing milkmaid on the wheel of a German clock. Now he saw she was made of many different parts, and each one was likely to go flying off with enough pressure. The force of having the baby in the middle of their kitchen must have snapped her head loose.

"It's dusty down here," her head told him. It had rolled behind the couch and, as such, was a little muffled.

Once or twice, he imagined her neck as one big 'ol screw where she would fasten a different head each morning. Some of her heads were kinder than others. He liked the one that stood behind him and whispered her wishes for his good day before he went to work, the one who licked the skin of his earlobe. He was not as fond of the one who told him she was tired. He, too, was tired. Everyone was tired. It was not worth mentioning.

"I wish I could see you," her head said. "Is that the baby crying?"

There should have been more blood. When he accidentally nicked his neck with a letter opener one winter ago he bled all over their wooden floor. The head she wore that day did not like those stains one bit. Her neck must have been drained of all her red, because when he looked down the hole on the top of her torso, he only saw darkness, like a whirl of shadows. It made him nauseous. Or maybe the eggs made him nauseous. She'd cooked them too quickly, and they were a tad runny for his liking.

He did the only thing he could think of to do: he snagged her head from behind the couch, placed her on the mantle and wrapped the baby in furs.

"I still can't see my family," said Mama's head, her voice a little weaker than it was before. "Where did you go?"

Dada tried to feed the baby the rest of his breakfast, but like its mother, the baby did not like eggs. They dribbled down its chin in a yellow spittle. Mama told him, using her helpful voice, which sounded less like a suggestion and more like rusting nails, that babies don't eat solid foods.

"Put the baby back," she said, adding that he was doing it wrong when he held the baby up to her eyes. "I miss you both." He placed the child in her stiff arms and uncovered her left breast, but the baby shook its head so hard Dada feared it, too, would pop off.

"Not there," Mama said in a whisper. "Give me my family back."

At a loss, Dada held the baby over the hole where her head should have been. The baby fit into the space of her neck just fine, so Dada turned the baby round and round until it snapped down into the pit of her and was swallowed by the darkness. He leaned over her to try to see where the baby had gone, and once his face was aligned with that dark swirl, Mama's arms grasped him around the shoulders and lifted him up into her as well. He dropped into those shadows headfirst, screaming all the way. Mama sighed her contentment on the mantle and closed her eyes.

Girl Teeth

The other kids got coins for their bones, but when my little sister's teeth fell out, my grandfather snatched them up before she could put them under a pillow. He kept them in a leather bag tied to his waist until he had the full set. The last one, a canine, fell out right before her sixth birthday with a plop. His gnarled hand trembled under her mouth, and he croaked with glee and rubbed it between his wrinkled fingers and muttered how strange it was they had fallen out so soon. My own gummed-in until I was twelve and a quarter, and I had the mint under my pillow to prove it. That night, he went into the yard and dug a little hole. In the morning, the bag around his waist was gone, poof, like he never had it at all. Little sister wailed for her teeth back, because she'd grown at least thirty coins by her estimation, and there was a dolly in a window she spied months back. But no matter how much she pleaded, and how much she made her voice the screech of a banshee, and how much wet she could scrounge up under her eyes, he would not tell her where they were. All he would say was my sister had not been truest-blue, and there were consequences to fibbing. When I asked what he meant, he said he had seen her throwing rocks at the steel bear traps we used to catch our breakfast and dinner, and they'd shut their teeth when there was no meat in their maw. Why else would my sister's teeth fall out so soon if she'd had flesh to chew? Those little bones were hungry, and hungry things bite unless they were buried. When I could not stand little sister's wet fish-face anymore, I went into her room and took her to the window and pointed out the little lump of disturbed earth where her bones were placed. She hooted and wanted to go out there and pull them out of the earth, but it was raining, and I told her to let them soak a bit first, like the roots of a sunflower, and we would get them in the sunlight. She smiled up at me and said I was being silly-willy and went out her window into the dark. In the morning, my mother stirred raisins into porridge and told me she was sorry there was nothing heartier. The wolves had eaten all the rabbits outside. I ate it happily until I heard a holler from my grandfather's room and ran to his door. He sat on his bed holding his hand to his face. There were marks on his skin, ugly little indents, red and pink, and weeping trails of blood running to his elbow. My mother put her hands on her face and asked what took a bite, but he said he did not know. Behind me, my sister grinned ear-to-ear, and said it must have been a beast.

A Girl, A Bird,
A Rocket to the Moon

No matter how much Wren stomped her feet and flailed her arms and told her parents it was illegal and she'd have them arrested as soon as she found an officer who didn't laugh at her, they grabbed her elbows at the first of every month and dragged her to the red brick building with the cartoon toothbrush with braces and gleaming white teeth. Her parents refused to believe that the orthodontist was anything other than the short balding man who politely answered all their questions about straight molars and pink gums. They always left the room before he transformed into an eighteen-foot-high monster. Then he'd get sick thrills by shoving his hands into the mouths of young kids and yanking on the metal he cruelly wrapped around their teeth. He had great big hairy arms and a voice like an eagle. He smelled like wet, soggy salt.

"This is cruel and unusual," said Wren, dragging the heels of her black and white shoes. She'd learned that phrase in school and used it on everything from vegetables to teeth to homework. "You can't make me go in there again."

Her parents made her go inside and sit in the plastic chairs in the waiting room. They held her arms down as Wren squirmed and tried to bite them.

"Wren," said her mother, her smile stretching her lips thin. "Not in public."

"Not at all," said her father. He turned pages of a magazine with one hand and rested the other heavily on Wren's shoulder.

A woman in matching blue pants and shirt came out of the monster's lair and called Wren's name. The woman looked at Wren and her face firmed up.

"Oh," she said. "Hi, again."

"You're one of his," said Wren.

Wren decided, if she was to face this monster time and time again, she wouldn't let him see her cry. Even Gizmo, the blackbird with the pink beak who lived on her sill, explained that monsters can't hurt you if they don't know you're afraid of them. He was always saying, "Wren, you have to be brave. Be as brave as you can be."

So Wren held her head up high and stiffly as she walked into the small room with the huge chair and the metal tray that held thin torture instruments: pokers and pinchers and slicers and mincers.

The monster man came in with his arms covered in the plastic he had taken to wearing ever since the time Wren drew blood.

He asked, "How have you been, Wren? Teeth okay?"

"I'll eat your fingers," said Wren.

He jammed his fingers in her mouth and felt all around her teeth and gums. He tightened the tiny screw on her braces. The metal pulled on her teeth and scrunched them together until her entire mouth vibrated in sharp pain. Wren tried to bite his hands but he moved too quick for her, and the woman in blue would pinch her gently on the upper arm whenever Wren caught his pinkie between her incisors.

Her parents never believed her about the monster man, no matter how much she sobbed and said it hurt, hurt, hurt even long after they had left the lair. This visit was proving to be no different than any of the others, so Wren covered her eyes with her hands the whole way home so that they couldn't see the water.

Her parents were tough to be around sometimes. They always smiled at her, and while Wren liked to smile, she also knew that she didn't like smiling all the time. Sometimes she liked frowning, or laughing, or crying. Often, she wanted to do all of these things at once. But her parents, they only had smiles. Warm smiles, cold smiles, stretched to their ears smiles, and smiles that were so small it was almost like they weren't smiling at all. The only difference between them was that when her father smiled he always opened his mouth so she could see his tongue and the dangly bit at the back of his throat. But when her mother smiled she never opened her mouth and, if by chance something inside her made her so happy she couldn't help but show all those teeth and tongue and gums, she'd put her hand over her lips and look at her feet.

Gizmo couldn't smile, what with his beak and all, so when he was happy he raised his wings above his head, pushed his feathery butt out as far as he could and pooped a white and black turd.

"You're gross," Wren always said whenever he was happy, but secretly she was jealous that she couldn't poop every time she was happy, too.

But Gizmo wasn't ever happy when Wren was crying, so when she came home and ran into her room Gizmo shuffled his feathers into a tight ball, balanced on Wren's thigh and held his smooth, cool beak under her chin. Because she could not fall asleep with her teeth thrumming, Gizmo stayed up with her the whole night.

Wren avoided her parents for as long as she could, which was only until morning when they knocked on her door and asked her down to breakfast.

"Waffles," they said cheerfully. "With blueberries. Your favorite."

Wren grudgingly followed them downstairs and sat at their table and ate the creamy,gooey waffles with the sugared blueberries they had made, but she refused to look at them or talk to them, even when she could feel their smiles looking at one another and struggling to stay in place.

Later, Wren was sitting in her room running her hands over Gizmo's soft feathers when she heard her mother say her name. Curious, she crawled on her hands and knees to the edge of the stairs and listened.

"Angry," her mother was saying. "All the time."

As carefully as she could, Wren tiptoed her way down. Gizmo spread his wings at the top of the stairs and beckoned her to come back.

"You're spying," accused Gizmo. "You wouldn't like it if someone did that to you."

"Shhhhhhh," said Wren. "It's about me."

But Gizmo dropped his beak to his chest and headed back into Wren's room. He stopped at the doorway and said, "It'll make you sad, and then I'll be sad with you."

"Oh shush," said Wren.

"Why must you look for an excuse to break our hearts," said Gizmo, then ruffled his feathers and hopped up onto his sill.

Wren rolled her eyes and turned back to her mother.

"Don't know what to do," her mother said and lapsed into silence. Then she said, "twenty or so more visits. She fights us every time."

And then, "doesn't know what's good for her."

Wren ran back into her room and slammed the door, not caring who heard.

"Did you hear, Gizmo?" she asked. "They're going to make me keep going back to that horrible monster!"

"Well yes," said Gizmo. "That's how braces work. It's to bind your teeth together so they don't fall out. Everyone gets it done these days."

"Everyone," grumbled Wren.

Gizmo was right. The next day at school Wren looked closely at the mouths of the kids in her class and everywhere she saw the familiar gleam on their teeth.

Monsters have gotten all of us, thought Wren, and felt a heaviness in her chest for her classmates. She gathered them around her at recess on the hot blacktop and told them she understood their pain, their monthly agony that kept them up in the nights and how parents refused to understand.

"Let's go," she told them, "to Africa. We can discover the baby of a lion and a giraffe. A Liraffe, or a Girion. We'll be famous and can do whatever we want, then."

But her peers only stared at her dumbly or laughed, then they wandered off and ran around in circles, something they loved to do but which Wren never really saw the point of.

When she told her teachers about Africa, they said animals can't mate like that.

"But it's far away," Wren said. "You don't know everything that happens there."

"Yes, we do," said her teachers, and handed her several books on the subject.

Wren read each line and grew heavy because it sure seemed like the books did know everything about Africa.

"I've got to get away from here on my own," Wren told Gizmo later that day as they sat on top of the stairs and listened to her parents bang out a dinner in the kitchen. She said, "I have to go somewhere that's new and nobody knows anything about."

"No place like that left," said Gizmo. "Everything on Earth is all found out."

Wren pushed her forehead against the railing on top of the stairs and rubbed her cheek where the braces nicked the soft skin. She heard her parents smiling downstairs and felt her stomach bunch up like dirty laundry.

"Then I'll have to move," she told Gizmo. "I'll move up, up, up."

She told Gizmo her plan to escape and live on the moon, the one place her smiling parents could not follow and where nobody she knew had braces. And, more importantly, she knew monsters could not breathe in space.

Though he poo-pooed the idea up and down her room, Gizmo brought her all kinds of thingamabobs he found on his daily flights to help her build a Rocket-To-The-Moon-Rocket. She didn't know where he found these things, but he brought all sorts of gewgaws and thingys and even managed to find a long, thin doodad with wires coming out of both ends.

She had to ask her father if she could borrow his screwdriver and hammer and wrench.

"I'm building a rocket," said Wren and lowered her eyes to her socks.

"That's wonderful," said her father, beaming. "I always wanted to be an astronaut, myself."

The next day he gave her his tools and a stack of books from the library with pictures of long white shuttles with their butts exploding in fire as they zoomed straight up to the lining of the sky. She showed Gizmo the pictures and said she needed parts that looked just like that: white and smooth and able to pierce the atmosphere.

She furiously worked at shaping the things Gizmo gave her into something that looked like it was from the book.

The doohickey was delicate because the thin, copper tubes that made up its long body were super bendy, and the red and green and blue and purple wires that burst out of its head like fireworks gave off little shocks if they touched other metals. It needed to be slowly bent around the whatchamacallit which was so big it was taking up almost all of her bedroom. The whatchamacallit was a block of metal so large that when Gizmo brought it to her he had been so impressed with his own birdy strength he shat all over her bedroom in glee. The whatchamacallit held the fuel and once the Rocket-To-The-Moon-Rocket started firing up the fuel would roll around and spurt into the doohickey, and that would send all that energy and spurty-power into the rocket and take her up, up, up.

Gizmo was the one who told her the doohickey couldn't be tightened all at once. It was the same excuse her parents gave her when she said that if the braces were tightened really hard just the one time Wren would already have the stupid perfect teeth they wanted her to have. And, she wouldn't have to be in pain at the beginning of every month. Even though they explained that that isn't how teeth worked she knew they were silly. They were in real estate and that had, as far as Wren was concerned, nothing to do with teeth. But Gizmo was a bird and he had no teeth. No teeth meant he was trustworthy.

With her father's wrench and hammer and the screwdriver with the flat head she furiously formed all the contraptions into something that looked like it was from the book. She had to hide it under her bed every morning so that her parents wouldn't find it and spoil her plans.

But her parents were nosy and always liked being in her business. They knocked on her bedroom door and she could hear them smiling at her. "Wren," they said, "don't you want breakfast? Even astronauts get hungry."

"I'm very, very busy," Wren said.

"Wren, darling, it's time for a shower. We can smell you through the door. You're one little greaseball monkey."

"I'm busy!"

"Wren, darling. You have to go to school."

"No, I don't."

"You do. It's the law," they said, and she could hear their smiles tremble.

"That's silly," said Wren.

Her parents started to push their way into Wren's room, and even though Wren and Gizmo barricaded themselves against the door and pushed back with all their might, Wren's parents were much stronger. It was her father that overcame Wren and Gizmo's strength, and he pushed the door so hard that Gizmo rolled all the way under the bed, and Wren fell to her stomach.

"You can't shut us out Wren," her father said, wrapping his large arms around her small frame and resting his smile on her shoulder. He added, "We are always going to be here for you."

"Bah," said Wren.

It took several days for Wren to properly bend the doohickey around the whatchamacallit without breaking it. She sent Gizmo out to look for Elmer's glue but even though he showed how his wings were falling out from flapping so hard he couldn't find any. So Wren put him to work making sure the veeblefetzer had enough dirt and water in it (that was the fuel to make the whole thing boom, boom, boom upwards and away) and that the thingamabobber was able to withstand all kinds of temperature, because that was what would heat up the veeblefetzer and make it all fly.

She was very confident in the science of her rocket.

Sneaking downstairs, she ran behind potted plants and dived into closets whenever her parents walked into her line of sight. She waited for them to go into another room before she scavenged in cabinets and threw pencils and pens and notebooks and calculators and brooms and the mop and even several coats onto the floor.

"Honey," said her mother, making Wren jump. "Can I help you find something?"

Mother was wearing her I'm worried about you smile, the kind that was all wobbly on one side.

"I need Elmer's glue," said Wren.

"Why didn't you just ask?" Her mother went and got a blue glue stick from a desk drawer in the kitchen and handed it to Wren.

"There's no cow on the label."

"It's just as good as any other," said her mother.

"Cow glue is the best," said Wren.

"It's all the same."

"Ughhhh," said Wren, and ran back upstairs.

"Wren!" shouted her mother. "You need to clean up the mess you made."

"I'm working on a top-secret rare assignment!" Wren shouted back and locked her door.

Over the next couple of days Wren concentrated on nothing else except getting herself into the air even though she was nervous that when she was up there it might get lonely, because one of the books said there was no sound in space. Still, she didn't want Gizmo to think that she didn't appreciate all the work he had done, and anyway, the Rocket-To-The-Moon-Rocket was rather fun to make with him.

"We need to get it done before the first of the month," said Wren. "Else they'll send me back to the monster." She rubbed her jaw and winced.

Wren managed not to get her parents to come into her room by showering early and being by the door when she had to go to school. The Rocket-To-The-Moon-Rocket was way too big to hide from them now. Her father bought it right away and smiled and ruffled her hair and said she was growing up, but her mother smiled tightly and narrowed her eyes. When Wren used the bathroom during breaks on the Rocket-To-The-Moon-Rocket she would catch her mother dusting the table in the hallway, the table her mother never dusted, and was very close to Wren's bedroom door.

When it only needed the final finishing touches, Wren and Gizmo smeared generic glue all over the gewgaws and spent the night sitting on them so that they would be firmly fixed in the morning. Then it would be ready for flight.

"I made a spot for you," said Wren. She pointed at the perch she glued next to the pilot seat, which was really just a stick Gizmo had brought in by accident one day.

"I can't go with you," said Gizmo. "I can't breathe all the way up there."

"But Giz," said Wren. "You have to go where I go. We're a team."

"But I can't," said Gizmo. "You want to go somewhere where no one else can follow."

He turned away from her and jumped on the sill.

Wren didn't know if she wanted to go to the moon all alone, even though she had to escape her aching teeth. Gizmo was the only one she knew who was not like any other of his kind, or her kind, and it was not only the pink beak that made him stand out, or that he could carry way more than he weighed, or even that he once tried to train her to poop when she was happy just like him. She wasn't even sure why she liked him so much, except that he seemed a part of her, if blackbirds with pink beaks could be a part of a little girl.

There was a soft knock at her door. "Wren," said her mother's watery smile. "I think you slept in. It's time for school."

"Uh," said Wren. "I'm very sick. Over 150-degree temperature. Cough. I better stay in bed. And you shouldn't come in or you'll get just as sick as I am."

"Wren," sighed her mother, "I know you hate the orthodontist, but that's no reason to miss school. In a few years you'll thank us for making you go, trust me."

"Doubt it," said Wren.

The knob of Wren's bedroom door caught on the lock. "Wren," said her mother, "you have to let me in."

"No, I don't."

Wren's mother called for her husband, and Wren ran to her window to get Gizmo to help her with the door, but Gizmo was gone. Not even a bit of his poop remained on the sill.

Wren's braces hurt more than they had ever hurt her before.

"Wren!" cried her father. "Please open the door."

"No!" said Wren. "You can't make me go to school and you can't make me go to the monster! I'm going to the moon!"

Wren hopped into her Rocket-To-The-Moon-Rocket and pushed the button that heated up the fuel in the veeblefetzer. She set her straight-o-meter to aim her at the moon and hurried it along because she could hear her father hitting his body against the door.

"Wren!" they said. "Wren, what do you mean?"

The gauge-o-meter that told her everything was filled up and ready to go began to beep and glow, so Wren pushed the button that started the explosion out of the butt and held on to her seat.

Just as the Rocket-To-The-Moon-Rocket began to lift off the ground, her father broke into her room and stumbled when he saw Wren in her machine. It was the first time Wren saw her parents without their smiles, and she realized how grown up they were.

Her parents grabbed onto each side of the Rocket-To-The-Moon-Rocket and held it down. It shook and whined in their grasp, but together they dug their heels into the plush carpet and whitened their knuckles over the wings. They said, "stop, Wren! You haven't done your homework! You haven't eaten dinner! You've got an appointment at the orthodontist!"

Wren looked at the straight-o-meter and it said if she didn't get off the ground right-at-this-moment-now she wasn't going to go straight to the moon, so she cried to her parents that they had to let go, or she wouldn't make it.

Her mother openly cried great big watery tears, and she cried with her mouth open. Wren saw that her mother's teeth were big and gapped. The spaces between the molars and incisors and front two were so large whole pieces or carrot or celery could fit in-between. Her mother had teeth just like Wren's own, except that her mother's weren't covered up with metal and wires. Wren wanted to say just how cool her mother's teeth were, and probably would be even beautiful if she ever showed them in a smile, but her mother saw Wren looking and slapped her hands over her mouth.

Alone, Wren's father couldn't hold down the Rocket-To-The-Moon-Rocket, and it burst out of his hands like a rabbit hops, jittery and with its legs kicking furiously at the air. Wren was pushed to the back of her seat when she blasted off from her room, breaking into and past the ceiling, and into the great big blue sky. She wanted to turn and say goodbye to her parents but she couldn't turn her head. So she opened her mouth to scream her farewells but the pressure was so great she couldn't form a single sound. The air was so thick and hot that when she pushed her head forward against it she felt the braces on her teeth begin to come undone.

First the small bits of metal bent and twisted against her teeth, but her teeth were slimy from her spit so they screeched and slid off the white part like they were rolling down a slide. Then they formed into a small scratchy ball on her tongue, all that metal torture, and Wren could taste the gritty cement-glue. She rolled it to the front of her teeth with her tongue and spit it out. It landed against the front of the cockpit. Wren ran her tongue across her teeth and her gums, and though she could feel the bumps of the glue at the edges where the tooth met gum, for the first time in a long time her mouth didn't hurt at all, and she smiled wider than her parents ever did.

She looked down below her and saw that the world was really truly blue and big. She couldn't even see her house, it was all a blur. She strained her eyes hard at the world and thought, maybe, that tiny little speck of pink there was Gizmo flying around looking for parts for something else they would have made, or maybe he was looking for her, or maybe he was saying toodle-hoo.

The pink speck faded into the big blue, and Wren felt, in her stomach, the pressure drop away from all sides of the Rocket-To-The-Moon-Rocket. But when the pressure dropped away so did everything around her. It started as a small vibration, then went into full out shakes. Outside she could see the gewgaws begin to tear away from one another. She cursed that she had not insisted on the Elmer's Glue, because the cow on the front of the package was reliable. Once the gewgaws fell away the doodads went next, because they were made out of wire and black feathers. Then the whatchamacallit simply dropped out the bottom back to earth, and then everything else fell away except for Wren, who kept on floating and floating towards the moon.

This is better than Africa, supposed Wren, who looked out into space and thought what a grand adventure it was going to be, especially when she discovered all those girions and laraffes who, if they didn't live on earth, probably lived on the moon.

It was interesting, thought Wren, and new, to not hear a thing at all in space. It was vast and quiet, and she didn't feel anything except for a little tinge in her mouth. She stuck her fingers in, cringed, and out came a little bit of blood from where the braces had scratched the side of her tongue.

Acknowledgements

This book is dedicated to my three nieces, who must navigate the strangeness of being alive. May your journey be full of wisdom and growth that is kind to you. Please don't read this book until you are older.

These words would not have existed without the continuous, loving support of my mother and father. Special thanks to those who have navigated words alongside me: Misha Rai, Michelle Zuppa, LaTanya McQueen, Colette Arrand and many others. I want to especially thank my husband, Nathan Riggs, who reads Aesop's Fables to fall asleep, and who asks me what I dreamed during the night.

The following stories were previously published with slight variations in the following places:

"The Candy Children's Mother" at Okay Donkey

"The Skins of Strange Animals" at Story

"Egest Leporidae" at Spider Road Press

"They All Could Have Loved You Until You Ate That Child" at Juked

"In the Belly of the Bear" at The Golden Key

"How One Girl Played at Slaughtering" at Ginko Tree Review

"The Mother Left Behind" at Gone Lawn

"An Old Woman with Silver Hands" at Smokelong Quarterly

"A Bird, A Girl, A Rocket to the Moon" at Pink Narcissus Press

"A Girl Without Arms" at Pink Narcissus Press

"Home Belly Wants" at Pindeldyboz

"Mama Floriculture" at Pink Narcissus Press

"A Woman With No Arms" at Wigleaf

"Get Bent" at Gargoyle

"Match Girl" at Variant Literature

"Girl Teeth" at Pidgeonholes

About the Author

Angela Wood

A.A. Balaskovits is the author of *Magic for Unlucky Girls* and *Strange Folk You'll Never Meet*. Her work has been published in *Best Small Fictions*, *Indiana Review*, *The Missouri Review*, *Story* and many others. Find her on Twitter @aabalaskovits and at aabalaskovits.com

Also from A.A. Balaskovits

"*Magic for Unlucky Girls* is that rarest of things: a book that doesn't remind me of anything else I've read ... A wonderful, truly original work."
— Emily St. John Mandel, author of *Station Eleven*

"To say that the stories in *Magic For Unlucky Girls* are unsettling is an understatement. In these tales, A. A. Balaskovits has created characters and worlds we think we know, and then destroys our expectations-unflinchingly, with no gory or sordid detail spared, and often with alarming violence. Yet, despite kicking us out of our collective comfort zone, these stories go down like pleasant poison, with language that moves seamlessly between brutal starkness and hypnotic lyricism. Balaskovits takes the stories that form the core of us from childhood and reshapes them into something dark and unfamiliar. Magic For Unlucky Girls is a bold debut from a bold author, and make no mistake— these are stories that matter, and that will stick with you long after you've read them."
— William Jablonsky, author of *The Indestructible Man: Stories* and *The Clockwork Man*

About Santa Fe Writers Project

SFWP is an independent press founded in 1998 that embraces a mission of artistic preservation, recognizing exciting new authors, and bringing out of print work back to the shelves.

  @santafewritersproject | @SFWP | at www.sfwp.com